FOREST THINGS

Also by
GERALD DiPEGO

With a Vengeance

GERALD DiPEGO

FOREST THINGS

DELACORTE PRESS/NEW YORK

Published by
Delacorte Press
1 Dag Hammarskjold Plaza
New York, N.Y. 10017

Manufactured in the United States of America
First printing

Designed by Oksana Kushnir

Library of Congress Cataloging in Publication Data

DiPego, Gerald.
    Forest things.

    I. Title.
PZ4.D596Fo [PS3554.I63] 813'.5'4   79–311
ISBN: 0–440–02338–6

Are the ancient myths only stories fashioned in the minds of men and retold a thousand times? Are they actual events that took place in some distant age, or are they eternal life-plays that are enacted again and again wherever there are deep mists and tall trees and other forest things?

Bright mountain moon only half-buttoned through the sky. This night was in a hurry, and Til watched as it spread and fell like a dark blanket across his lap. Til Sharkis, named for a mountain, sat with his legs dangling down Whitestone Cliff, big boots floating over four hundred feet of August air. "Long way down," he said, and scraped a three years' depth of fallen needles from the forest floor, held them and dropped them over the cliff edge. The wind blew them back. "Would you blow me back if I fell over? Hm?" He laughed, and the wind blew back his laughter.

He looked up to see torn scraps of clouds busy among the stars. "What's the rush?" Sunset had been just a flash of pink and gone. The stars had popped on all at once from a single throw of the switch. Til stood up full against the warm wind. "Getting ready to put on a show? Going to rain on me, or what?" The wind only hummed to itself, busy spreading and shaking the trees. Til stretched, let the heavy gusts rock him on the cliff edge. His yawn ended in a shout. Then he sang, stepping about, made restless by the motion of the forest and the sky.

He wanted to run. He had run at night before. It was dangerous. It had always ended in a fall. By day he could sail through the forest, running at top speed, his eyes finding places for his feet, his feet scarcely touching the forest floor. But this was night, and the moon was small. He should walk up the trail to his cabin, or walk down the mountain to the lakeside resort where he had a room waiting for him. He should walk.

FOREST THINGS
—————
1

He was running without even thinking about it, running and smiling and chasing the wind among the trees. Down. He had decided to go down to the resort, because the lodge roof didn't leak like his cabin did, because in the lodge was Mrs. Rendon, and she would hear him come in, and, in a while, she would drift to his room like a sleepwalker, drift to his bed. He wanted her tonight. He did not want to lie alone while the sky partied and the forest danced.

He ran, and the feeling began. He was light, so light, and so swift, he was almost not there at all. He was a boy again, running through this same forest with his father, the man ten strides ahead, the two of them growing lighter, lighter, the soles of their shoes scarcely touching the ferns and the needles and the earth.

Floating. He would soon be floating. He had never been this close before.

Daddy! "I know," his father shouted, and they both laughed, giddy with it, with the flying. "I know!" And he swore his father's shoes stopped touching at all. He swore it.

So fast. A fall now could break his bones, even kill him, and it was night. Still he ran, and he laughed, giddy with it.

Daddy! Wait! His father, ten strides ahead, flying, turned and smiled and disappeared.

But this was night, and the moon was gone, and still he ran, no little boy now, heavier than his father had been, and still almost floating. Almost. He dodged the dark trunks, somehow sailed over fallen trees, missed the tangled shrubs, ran on and picked up speed, gaining on the wind.

He laughed deep inside his chest. His body flashed among the trees, whisked down the mountain. His powerful legs felt no strain, his arms were held out for balance. His feet were ready to stop touching at all, ready now. . . .

He took flight.

For the first time, he felt no earth beneath him. He ran, but his boots tread on nothing. He flew, and he cried deep inside his chest, and he realized—he had not caught the wind. He was the wind.

GERALD DI PEGO

Tilima Lodge was on the shore of Lake Tilima at the foot of Mount Tilima of the Adirondack chain. The lodge offered eight rooms, but one was occupied by the owner, the Widow Edith Rendon, and one was reserved for the handyman, Til Sharkis. The other six were empty now. There were also four cabins for rent, spread across the clearing between forest and lake. Only one cabin was rented. The Chase family had come two days ago. Louis Chase and his wife, Patti, were in the small kitchen, speaking quietly about tomorrow's hike and will it rain, and if so, what would they do stuck in the cabin all day? In the living room their thirteen-year-old son, Allan, was asleep, and their daughter, Lyn, sixteen, was just now being drawn from the bed to the window by the rhythms and wild songs of the night.

She stood watching with hands flat on the cool glass, and she hoped for a storm, hoped for the sky to break and fall in giant pieces, with terrible sounds, and the wind to scatter the trees like leaves and tear the cabin from the earth and set it spinning. When it stopped, the world would be changed. She asked for a storm.

The dark treetops nodded. Agreed. The pitch of the wind rose to a scream. Lyn held her breath. The earth shook. Something was moving through the forest, moving closer. She heard the rush of it like a great gust, racing from the center of the storm, directly toward the cabin, toward her. She stopped blinking, locked her eyes on the dark forest, and the forest moved, leaped for her.

She stepped back and nearly shouted, but it was a man, a man had burst from the forest and run past her window, run

FOREST THINGS

———
3

into the clearing near the lodge. She watched as he slowed and stopped and fell to his knees, his body heaving with great breaths, his head held down, then brought up and back until his face was parallel to the sky. He smiled. He laughed, but she heard only the wind.

In a moment, he rose and began to walk to the lodge, and she recognized him now. He was the man who worked there. She didn't know his name.

She put her hand on her thin T-shirt, pressed it between her breasts, felt her heart made wild. But the wind was down to moaning again, and the trees only swayed. She wondered if the storm was over and if anything had changed.

Til walked on shaky legs to the dark lodge. He stopped on the porch a moment, sat on the steps, still out of breath. It had been the best run, the very best ever, and it had been at night. He smiled. He wanted to tell someone. I ran tonight, and I didn't fall. And listen . . . after a while I wasn't running anymore. I was above. Above. He rose and walked into the lodge, let the screen door slap closed behind him.

He walked heavily toward his room, knowing she would hear. Through her sleep she would hear him. He entered the tiny room and lit the lamp. They used kerosene at Tilima Lodge and firelight and as little electricity as possible. Mrs. Rendon was a saving soul. He twisted the lampwick down very low, sat on the bed. His breath was back, and the sweat was coming now. He took off his shirt and wiped himself with it, took off his boots and heavy jeans and dropped them loudly

GERALD DI PEGO

4

on the floor. He stripped the spread and quilt from the bed, lay on the sheet and waited.

He listened to the last of the wind, only a whisper now. The sound chilled him, like a voice, and he thought of his father. You knew, didn't you. He spoke to the memory, the man ten strides ahead, turning, smiling at his son. Dad, you knew about the wind—that you don't catch it. He listened for another whisper, but he heard the creak of a bed, a footstep. She was coming.

Edith Rendon, her eyes closed, took another step away from her bed, touching the wall for support and direction. She moaned slightly with each quick breath. She seemed in pain. She seemed asleep, struggling in a dream.

She was a tall woman, erect and firm at fifty-two, long-limbed with large hands and feet, large breasts dancing wildly under her thin gown as she moved across the room. Her graying hair was loose about her shoulders and tangled in her face. She blundered toward the door, opened it, her moaning louder, her breath faster now. She lunged into the hall and hurried over the worn carpet, touching the walls, brushing the wall now to find the open door.

She rushed through that door, her moans sharp outcries now. Her eyes were still closed, yet her body moved forward unafraid, vulnerable, blind.

She felt herself caught at the waist by two strong hands, the fingers pressing hard, pressing warmly through the gown. She was eased on to a bed. She lay on her back, her breath coming in whimpers now, her chest heaving. She felt those hands at

FOREST THINGS
———
5

her knees, moving slowly upward, strong fingers rubbing her thighs, pushing the silky cloth ahead of them, baring her to the waist. Her breath and body trembled together. Her hands went into her hair and made fists. She wept.

Those fingers stroked her soft inner thighs, brushed upward to where the moisture began, then pressed, and her legs gave way, moving apart. She felt a body now, hairy as a beast, easing down on her, legs between her legs, warm breath on her neck, a hand like a claw scratching at her shoulder strap, pulling, tearing it down to uncover her breast, then fondling, pinching. She wept in whispers and moans, her trembling shaking the bed. She felt lips on her breast, sharp teeth on her nipple and a stiff, thick penis probing, pushing, entering her.

Her fists opened and she grabbed blindly, held that strong sweating body to her own. They rocked together in a great heaving of muscles, stretching and slacking of limbs, thrusting of loins, in a quickening rhythm that threatened to crack the bed and sunder the walls around them.

She stiffened and caught her breath, frozen a moment, held in the fierce grip of something she could not see, trapped in the private darkness inside her eyes—then she cried out, feeling herself dying, melting, flesh and bone dissolving in a warm river that ran between her legs. There were no bodies, no bed. There was only that fluid, no longer a river, but still now, a pool.

Til straddled her and rose up on his knees, still inside of her. Her limp hands covered her breasts. Her eyes were closed loosely now, peacefully, tears shining on her cheeks in the low lamplight.

GERALD DI PEGO

6

He withdrew from her and lay on his side, watching her. He was not supposed to speak. He was supposed to allow her to believe she had dreamed him; she had not come to him; she had not even risen from her own bed. He knew this, though she had never told him. He had learned by speaking to her at first, trying to make her answer, make her open her eyes and see him. She would not, and in the morning she would not speak of it. It was not something that happened. It was a dream. She was a widow. She needed no man. She kept faithful to a memory. She only dreamed.

She turned on her side and slowly swung her long legs out of the bed. She stood, and the skirt of the gown dropped from her waist, covered her buttocks and legs. Her hands, soft and weak now, lifted the silky material to her breasts, lifted the straps to her shoulders.

Wait, he wanted to say, wait. Sit on the bed. "Just sit and listen," he said. "You don't have to talk. Please."

He had torn one strap of the gown. The material dropped down, uncovering her breast. She placed her hand over it, took a step away from the bed, eyes still closed.

"I ran tonight," he said.

She drifted silently out of the room, drifted down the hall. In a moment he heard the creaking of her bed. She would fall asleep now, hide in sleep, angry at him for speaking, angry about the torn strap. She would mend it in the morning.

He sat in his bed for a long while, then he shouted. "I ran tonight and didn't fall!" He got out of bed and began putting on his clothes, moving quickly. "Hear me?" Anger stretched his voice thin. "Can you say one goddamn word?" He put on his boots and clumped to the front door, stopping to shout back into the house. "I don't give a shit about the nightgown!"

The night had stopped moving. His steps on the porch were loud in the windless clearing. The lake lapped softly at the pier; an animal rooted at the woodpile; the sky was clear and innocent, as though it had never rioted at all.

Til turned his anger toward the creature at the woodpile, probably a raccoon. He jumped off the porch, hoping to give

FOREST THINGS

7

the animal a fright, watch him run panicked from woodpile to forest, but the rooting continued. He walked slowly, his hands in his back pockets, strolled around the corner of the lodge to the sheltered woodpile. "Boo, goddamnit."

A black bear rose up from the pile, stood on his back legs, leaned on the wood for support, a tall bear, larger than most. The animal's left ear was missing, along with a patch of fur, a new but dry wound. The eyes were clear and strong on Til.

Til drew his hands from his pockets and let them fall to his sides, straightening his body to full height and finding himself shorter than this giant, this forest dragon with scimitar claws and eyes as black and moist as his own. Til stared hard at those eyes, and he took a step closer, not away. He leaned into the teeth and claws and bulk of the beast and studied it with deep fascination. "One day . . ." he whispered. The bear blinked, only half interested. Til stepped even closer, deeper into the smell, the breath and the being of the great bear. He swallowed and sang in a whisper. "One day as Fiddlin' Dan went out to play, he met a grizzly standin' in his way. He couldn't climb a tree. He had no gun. He couldn't fly away. He was scairt to run." The bear went back on all fours, sniffing near the wood. "Hey, goddamnit, listen." But the bear seemed not to care. "I ran tonight." The creature grunted, chasing a scent. "I ran so fast I think I took off. I really do. Hear me?"

The bear began to move away. Til suddenly roared, a man-bear roar that grabbed the night and shook it awake. Birds screamed and deserted their trees, animals scratched through the brush in blind getaways. The bear stopped and turned on Til, bared his teeth and growled a deep booming growl that seemed to come from the center of the earth. Til drew in a long breath and roared louder still. The bear stood up, waving his paws and roaring with him. An owl screeched. Lights went on in the Chases' cabin and the room of the Widow Rendon. A fierce smile jumped from Til's eyes like a spark. He trapped the laughter inside of him and turned back to the lodge as the bear lumbered off into the forest.

GERALD DI PEGO

8

Til closed the door quietly behind him and walked softly to his room, the silent laughter hurting his chest and bringing tears.

Til woke up cold, sitting up and snatching at the fallen quilt and spread, piling them on and snuggling under, digging with shoulders, elbows and knees, trying to burrow back into sleep. But the Widow Rendon was conducting in the kitchen, a morning song of sizzling grease and iron pans, squeaky oven door, running water, sounds that somehow turned into smells and came for him, found him under all those bedclothes—bacon, biscuits, coffee. He rose and dressed, went to the kitchen with his boots untied, the laces whipping and snapping as he walked.

He poured the coffee. She started the eggs. "Mornin'," he said. He had said that every morning they had breakfasted together over the past three years, and she had always answered, "And it's a fine one," or "And it's a poor one." But this morning she didn't answer at all, angry at him for speaking last night, angry about the strap of her gown, which he was sure was already mended.

"Mornin'," he said again, taking his seat. She turned to him, her eyes stern but so blue, magnetic blue, drawing the blue from her denim shirt, from the painted tiles on the kitchen wall, from the blue-willow bowl, from the sky at the window, pulling blue from everywhere and storing it and burning it in a low, even flame that warmed him, that softened her face in spite of her anger, made her pretty. He smiled and hid his

FOREST THINGS

smile in his coffee cup, sipped and burned his tongue. "Jesus!"

"Mind your language."

He spoke unintelligibly, fingering his tongue. "Burned myself."

"What?"

"I said, good mornin'."

She turned back to the eggs and he studied her straight back, her hair combed and rolled on her neck, her ass in faded jeans. If he touched her now, she'd kill him with an iron skillet to the skull, and that thought made him smile. He didn't know why.

"That Chase family builds fires morning, noon and night." She spoke to the eggs in the pan. "They use as much firewood as they do water. Better chop some more this morning."

Til was soaking his burned tongue in a glass of water. He withdrew it to answer. "Gonna teach them to chop their own. They like that."

"Sure. Then somebody chops off a foot and sues me." She served the eggs and sat across from him. They ate in silence. When she did speak, she didn't look at him. "I thought I was dreaming last night, but it turned out to be real."

He stopped still, his mouth open around a biscuit bite. He stared at her and waited and nearly choked. After three years of silence would she now admit that the Widow Rendon was a woman and Til Sharkis was a man and that sometimes they needed each other, sometimes they touched each other?

"Those bears scared me right out of my sleep."

Til washed the biscuit down, disappointed. He took another bite. "Bears?"

She stopped eating, looked at him. "You heard those bears."

He went on with his breakfast, innocent. "Last night? Nope."

She put her cup down hard. "They woke up the whole forest—now don't tease me, Sharkis."

"You must've been dreamin'."

GERALD DI PEGO

10

"I was sitting up wide awake!"

He shrugged, eating as he spoke. "Some people sit up while they're dreamin'. Some even walk around the house." He saw her going pale, holding her breath. "They say that if you speak to a sleepwalker, you scare 'em to death. I don't agree. I think they just don't hear you, keep right on walking, like you're not there at all." He rose, bringing his plate and cup to the sink, feeling her eyes hot on his back. "Now me, I'm different. When I sleep, I sleep. I don't move around. I guess it would take somebody coming over and jumping right on me to wake me up . . ."

"Sharkis!"

"Mm?" He rinsed his dishes, watched the water carry away his crumbs and his coffee, and he wondered if it was all over now—three years of this tall, strong woman sleepwalking to his bed at night and denying him in the morning with her eyes, with her tone of voice.

"We're talking . . . about bears." Her voice had gone thick and moist. He turned to her and saw how her anger had mixed with fear.

"Are we?"

"Yes." Her words were soft, separated for emphasis. "They . . . were . . . real. And you heard them."

I love your ass, he wanted to say. I love your breasts—even right now. Right now I want to open your shirt and touch them. I love your body and your eyes. If only, when you come to me at night, you would let me see your eyes. It would be better. We'd be even better. We'd break the bed. We'd laugh and cry and you wouldn't be ashamed. "Mrs. Rendon," he said.

"What?" The corners of her mouth trembled slightly.

"I chased him away so you could go back to sleep."

"Who?" It was a whisper.

"The bear. It was only one."

"Oh." Her eyes shimmered with sudden moisture. Til came close, leaned on the table in front of her.

"And when he refused to leave, I bit off his ear."

FOREST THINGS
———
11

She leaned an elbow on the table and brought her hand to her forehead. "Well, I thank . . ." She had to stop a moment. "I thank you for driving off all the bears and lions. Now how about chopping some firewood before you go to town?"

"Yep." And he moved for the back door.

She squeezed her eyes closed and in that sudden darkness she felt the grip of a beast, strong arms and legs pressed to her body, joining her body. She felt fear and then desire and then shame. She opened her eyes at the bang of the screen door. He was gone.

Til chopped wood, glancing now and then at the Chases' cabin. The two children were watching him from the porch and pretending not to watch him. They came down the steps, looking about and moving toward him and pretending not to move toward him.

"Hiya." He kept his eyes on the log, heard them murmur an answer. They came close, but looked off at the lake, up at the wooded mountain. He studied them with glances. Shy kids, quiet kids, both of them thin and long and growing longer. The girl was wearing shorts, and Til saw thighs as rich and ready as any woman's, legs that shined, tight, smooth flesh.

Each time he raised the ax, he brushed his eyes over her for an instant before swinging the blade into the wood. He saw a delicate neck once, and once a straight little chin. He caught sight of the soft mounds on her sweatshirt, made by small young breasts. The shirt was short-sleeved, and on her upper arm he saw a mark and checked it again on the next swing. A

GERALD DI PEGO

12

birthmark, he imagined, faint purple lines, like fingers, a royal mark, a lost princess.

He saw long, fine, red-brown hair with sunlight and shadow trapped in the strands. He glimpsed a face that held him, made him miss his mark with the ax. He rested, staring openly now at her deep new eyes, eyes not even one-quarter full, eyes taking deep drafts of all that could be seen, serious and careful eyes of changing color, now blue-green, now gray, with feelings caught in the colors—shyness, curiosity, pleasure, embarrassment, and more, Til thought. There were smiles kept there, perhaps even loud laughter. There was joy, carefully covered. He wondered if she would ever unwrap it and show it to him.

Strength and shyness did battle in those eyes. She did not look away. "Did you hear those bears last night?" she said.

"God, woke us all up," the boy said. "My dad loaded his gun."

"Don't need a gun." Til chopped at the log.

"Why not? My dad said bears've killed people around here." There was a challenge in the boy's words.

Til kept working as he spoke. "Bears hate music."

The kids looked at each other, wondering.

"You meet a bear around here," Til said, "and it'll probably run away. If it doesn't you just sing to it." The children shared their own peculiar smiles, thin, twisted smiles, bent by lips afraid to loosen and to laugh, secret smiles. Til shrugged. "Works for me."

"Did you sing to the bears last night?" Her big, deep eyes were wondering. Til wanted to leap into them.

"Yep. There was only one." He paused. "I forgot your names."

"Lyn," she said. "And this is Allan."

"Hiya."

Allan nodded, staring off at his approaching parents with tension and without joy. Chase was a tall, hard-muscled man, his face sharply handsome and his eyes impatient. Til looked

FOREST THINGS

at Mrs. Chase to see if he could find the girl there. He found the same delicate neck and shoulders, light hair, long legs, but the face was wrong. The eyes were full and far away. He couldn't catch them.

"How about those bears," Chase said. "Battling right outside our door."

"Over by the woodpile," Til said, chopping again. "Only one—looking for mice." They all looked at the pile, as if the bear were there now.

"Sounded like he was on our porch," Mrs. Chase said.

Lyn gestured awkwardly with a lanky arm and hand, a self-conscious pointing at Til. "This man chased him away."

"My name's Til."

She flushed, embarrassed, but she said it. "He sang to it."

Mrs. Chase laughed. "What?"

"He sang to the bear, and it went away."

Til looked at the Chases and nodded solemnly.

Mrs. Chase laughed a halfhearted laugh, one high note hanging in the air, unsure. Mr. Chase flicked his eyes over Til, then turned and walked to the woodpile. Mrs. Chase followed him.

"Hard to believe," Allan said.

"Try it sometime." Til chopped through a log.

"Allan." Chase was calling his son to the woodpile. "Come and see what a bear track looks like."

Allan left. Til stared at Lyn. She looked away, but didn't leave.

"You know what a bear track looks like?"

She shook her head, no.

"You want to learn to chop wood?"

"Yes."

He handed her the ax.

"Lyn, come over here. Look at these tracks."

Her shoulders drooped. She leaned the heavy ax on the ground, and he took it back. She was half turned, leaving, when she said, "I saw you running last night." His reaction

GERALD DI PEGO

stopped her. She froze in that half turn. His look was so intense, so important.

"Did you see me fly?"

She stared at him with wonder. He slowly smiled and said the words exactly as if they were true.

"I ran so fast, I started to fly."

Her eyes answered his smile, warming, studying him. In a moment she turned and went to her family.

It was the noise of the outboard motor that pushed the boat across the lake. He was sure it wasn't the gas engine, wasn't the propeller. It was the unholy, ripping, mindless, stupid, screaming noise of the machine. Rowing would take hours each way. Even the canoe would take an hour and break his back besides. So twice a week he roared, buzzed, growled across the lake to the town of Tilima for mail and supplies.

Halfway across he almost always turned it off, killed the motor and let the lake and the sky, shredded by the sound, mend again. He switched the engine off now and lay back in the boat, let fingers dip into the cold water, let the lake drift under him and the sky meander above. The memory of the noise went on in his ears for a moment, even after sound and echo had gone. Then the memory too passed on, moving out across the lake, dwindling down to a hum that hit the horizon and shattered there. The wreckage floated for a moment and sank out of sight. The boat creaked; a loon laughed; the wind barely breathed.

The silence let him think, and thinking uncovered a raw

FOREST THINGS

spot in his mind, a wound forgotten and now sore. It was the picture of the Widow with her back to him, drifting out the door as he spoke to her. The raw spot stung as he passed over it. He flexed his strong shoulders, moved his head in an unconscious twitching as though he could physically avoid this thought. There was anger in his move, and panic. He feared what was coming. He made fists and ducked his head, but it was on him now, unshakable, and he was living again that day in the forest, the day of screams, when he had seen his father disappear and had shouted for him, searched for him until his boy-body ached and his boy-voice was all screamed away. By the time he had come down the mountain for help, he could no longer speak, and he had wept every tear he had.

They never found his father.

Til could not speak above a whisper for months. He was sent away to grow among strangers, a lost boy, forever drawn to his past and forever fighting off The Memory of the day of screams.

From the very first, the Tilima country had wanted him back. From the forest and the lake, from deep inside the stone center of Tilima Mountain, came a call the boy could hear but would not answer. He had been too deeply wounded. The pain overwhelmed the beckoning of the land, and he made up his mind he would never go back. He would go away.

He traveled across an ocean and back again. He wandered a scribble across the map, tracing a lacy pattern that slowed and rested but never stopped. He found places, but not his place. He rose above his pain, but found no joy. He was always in motion, and his motion was always away.

Through it all, the mountain called him still, and he began to listen. One day he answered: I was hurt there, more than I've ever been hurt—but I was happy there, more than I've ever been happy. I'll go home.

He came back. He made his peace with the Tilima country and with all of his past except one day, one Memory.

He would war against The Memory today using the com-

GERALD DI PEGO
———
16

pany of people as a weapon and maybe sex and surely laughter.

He pulled the cord and started the ungodly noise again, bearable only because it was pushing him across the lake to his friends.

Egon Webb made the sun dance on the lashes of his eyes. He squinted, blurred his vision, lowered his lids except for the smallest slits where his gray lashes quivered and made stars and diamonds, sunbursts and rockets, circles flecked with red, ringed in blue.

He sat on the main pier of Tilima Harbor, on a timber as cracked and weathered as he was, but the wood was a child compared with Egon. That timber was still a young tree when Egon Webb first walked these mountains, fished this lake, learned this forest.

"Gonna toss 'im in."

"Waylor?"

"Smells so bad. Jeeesus! Don't you ever change clothes, Egon?"

"Waylor, you paint that boat?"

"Who's that comin' in?"

He heard everything—the men speaking of boats, the man ridiculing him, the trucks in town, the loons over the lake and the motorboat that was too far away for the others to identify. He looked at the sun, and his eyes made rainbows. He spoke his first word in hours.

"Sharkis."

"What he say?"

FOREST THINGS

"He said, 'Sharkis.' "
"Til? Yeah, that's Til comin' in. How'd *he* know?"

Til stopped his motor and drifted the last ten yards to the pier, waving to Lyle Waylor, who fished for the restaurants, and Janz, who repaired boats, and the Berger brothers, who sold bait and tackle to the tourists.

"Sharkis."

"How's it goin'?"

"Look at that old fart. Hey, Til . . ." Tom Berger approached Til and stood beside him as he secured the boat. "Look at 'im." Berger was gesturing with his head, moving it to the side as though butting an invisible wall. "Look at him." Til followed the twitching of Berger's head and noticed Egon. "Sittin' there, sunnin' himself like a turtle. Let's toss 'im in."

Berger's brother laughed. Til stared at Egon. He had never joined in the ridiculing of the ragged man who had always been old, even when Til was a boy, when his father was a boy.

"I wouldn't care if the sun didn't heat 'im up and bring out the smell. Go near 'im and take a whiff."

Berger was speaking loudly enough for all to hear. The men chuckled as they worked. Til did walk closer to Egon, did smell his old clothes, old body, but he approached with reverence. Here was the man who knew the wilderness better than anyone, better even than Til's father had known it. Egon had somehow reached the secret heart of the forest and found something there that sustained him and no other. He was able to winter out there. Though no one had ever found a sign of a

GERALD DI PEGO
———
18

cabin or shelter or spotted a chimney or campfire, they knew that the old man lived in and with the forest all year. Not even the worst storms drove him into town. During each hard winter the people of Tilima would say, "This one killed off Egon. He's out there frozen someplace." But then he would appear, buy a few supplies, drink a whiskey in the bar, sleep in the park and then return to the forest.

Til saw that the old man wasn't sunning himself, those eyes were open a bit. He was staring at the sun, squinting as though he were trying to make out something written there. Til found himself following the old man's gaze. The sun blinded him for a moment. He looked at Egon, then tried to follow his eyes again.

"Doesn't it hurt your eyes?" He spoke only for Egon to hear. The man didn't move.

"Seen the bear?"

Til nodded. "One ear gone?"

"That's the one." The old eyes closed.

Til waited, then asked, "How'd he lose the ear?"

"Some fool shot him."

Til waited, wondered if there were more. Then he sighed and said, "He's a big one," and he felt foolish saying that. He felt like a talky townsman, a thousand miles from Egon and the heart of the forest. There had been no need to say it. They had both seen the bear. Egon had mentioned it, and they had remained in silence, sharing the fact of the tall, one-eared bear. He shouldn't have spoken. He began to move away.

"Don't say you've seen him."

"Why?"

But the old man didn't answer. The eyes became slits again, playing with sunlight. Til moved off.

Til entered the Clover Coffee Shop with two cheese-burgers sizzling on his mind. He knew exactly how they would smell and taste and feel against his teeth. He had them washed down with beer and digested by the time he was through the door.

The welcoming chant began, an automatic chorus of greetings from Dan and Emma Clover.

"Lookit Sharkis."

"We never see you anymore."

"Beard's in full now."

"Useta come in three, four times a week."

"How're things at the lodge?"

Til sat at the counter and did a slow spin on the stool, grinning at his welcomers, at Gil Coleman from the sawmill, in a corner booth, and mean Win Henderson at a table. He even grinned at a booth full of strangers, and when his revolving gaze swept over the new waitress, over tan legs and white uniform and braided hair, his boots touched the floor and stopped him. He stared, and behind him Emma leaned close and whispered.

"Susan."

Dan asked about the lodge and the Widow Rendon, Emma about the cheeseburgers. Til answered their questions, sipped his beer and watched Susan carry plates and wipe off tables, watched the white uniform stretch against her body, saw the outlines of her underwear and the curves of her legs and ass, followed the form of her neck and small shoulders. Bless their shoulders, he thought. Bless all their shoulders. I can feel them

GERALD DI PEGO
20

cupped inside my hands. Bless their soft swells of flesh and tender, tender nipples, pink and brown. Bless their legs. Bless their hands. He wanted to snuggle somewhere with Susan. She might be good or hateful, kind or cruel. He hadn't seen her eyes yet. But before he did, he blessed her for having braids and shoulders he could cup and bra straps and panties and rounded arms and smooth thighs and a vagina and hips and he imagined her sleeping, and he imagined her in the early morning, putting on her uniform and looking at herself in the mirror, and he loved her.

"There's another summer girl working at Elfon's." Emma moved in quick jerky motions, her head nodding nervously, thin hands placing napkin and silverware before him. She spoke in a low secret voice, a sly and dirty voice. "She ain't as pretty as Susan, though. Susan's got a nice little body, ain't she? Tight little socket for your plug." She laughed between her teeth, her arms jerking under the counter and producing a glass of water which she slid to him.

Emma was sixty or so, vaguely crippled, a slight stiffness of back and shoulder that robbed the smoothness from any move she made, broke that move into a series of twitches. She leaned close to speak in her dirty-joke voice. "Then there's always summer girls at Bishop's. You been out there? Who's your lady love now? I *know* you, Sharkis." Then more loudly as she twitched back to the grill. "You should come to town more. Summer's almost gone."

"He don't like it here."

Til spun around slowly to face mean Winston Henderson, and he smiled at the phenomenon, the ritual, the man leaning back and easing into it, revving up his mean thoughts and sliding into gear.

"He's got a future out there. How's that janitorial career comin' along?"

Winston was a big, wide man with too much belly. He was fifty and mostly bald under his gas-station cap. His uniform shirt and pants were stained so shiny in some places they ap-

FOREST THINGS

———

21

peared to be metal. The deep lines of his face looked as if they had trapped years of grease and grit. He smelled of motor oil and gasoline. It seemed to Til that Winston Henderson was slowly turning into a car.

"He ain't a janitor." Emma was defending him.

"What *do* you do out there, Sharkis?"

Til sipped his beer. "I keep away the bears and lions."

"You just can't take regular work."

"Regular?" Til shook his head sadly. He had worked as a mechanic in Winston's service station and still did now and then when the lodge was closed. "Just look at your hands, Win. Look at those fingers pounded flat, nails broken, old scars, new cuts. Cars'll do that to you. Cars are mean. They're always snapping at your fingers, growling, jumping for you. Takes a mean man to handle automobiles."

Winston muttered into his napkin. "Talking crazy, Sharkis."

Til had always thought of the machines as beasts, still hot and dripping as he worked beneath their bellies, powerful beasts that could crush him without ever knowing he was there. Over the years, he had learned to tame them, stroking them with his hands, feeling for the defect with his fingers or closing his eyes and listening to the voice of the beast and knowing what to touch.

"What'll you pay me, Winston? You know I'm the best there ever was."

"I want somebody who's gonna stay for more than three weeks at a time."

"That's my limit. After three weeks, the grease gets into my pores, and I can't breathe. I start turning into a real mean bad-ass like yourself. Do you remember being nice?"

Dan was chuckling. Emma brought Til his food and winked at him, sly again, dirty, speaking so only he could hear. "So who's your lady love now? Remember Laura last summer? She cried when she had to go back to school. She still write to you? So who's your lady love?"

He stared at her to stop her, to quiet her voice and hold her

GERALD DI PEGO
———
22

still. It took a moment. Emma was almost never still. He stared and waited, and she stopped. Then his eyes became gentle fingers, lightly brushing the hair back from her face, tracing her lips, smoothing lines of worry and age. She was a broken bird of a woman, a stick figure drawn with a fine point and sharp angles, caught in midflight for an instant, held by his eyes.

"You, Emma," he said.

A look flew up from her deepest place and rushed back again, darting like a dark bird back into shadow, then she laughed through her teeth and winked and moved away, but Til was shaken by what he had seen, by that glimpse of total desire and utter sorrow.

"Yes sir, you're the one, Sharkis. You got 'em comin' and goin'. Mostly comin'."

Her laugh went inside of him and lay heavily there, smothering his appetite. He tried to eat, but Emma's food did not equal the cheeseburgers made in his mind.

Deputy Stan Willis entered the Clover Coffee Shop and set off the automatic welcome.

"Lookit that Willis."

"The police are here in force."

"Take a load off."

"Who's in jail, anybody?"

"Gettin' fat, Stan."

Willis stood by the door. "On *your* food?" He joked without a trace of a smile. He surveyed the room with an even look that swept over the innocent, lingered on the unknown, challenged the possibles. He was a tall, stolid figure in blue, hung with straps and buckles and heavy revolver. His look had stopped on Til. Sharkis was definitely a possible. Sharkis in the right mood was a threat to persons and property. Sharkis had turned up in the middle of the wildest brawls in Tilima history and had written his name on the walls of both of the cells of the Tilima jail. Sharkis was peaceful today, and Willis moved his eyes along. When he was sure he owned the place, he

FOREST THINGS

walked toward the counter, sat next to Til, not looking at him, but poking him gently in the side.

"Stayin' out of trouble, Sharkis?"

"You should know."

Mean Winston Henderson joined them at the counter. "When you're ready to go after that bear, you just call."

The deputy nodded. "Maybe."

"What bear?"

"Got a marauding bear," the deputy said, rubbing his tired face.

"A killer," Henderson said.

Til turned to mean Winston. "Who got killed?"

Henderson ignored him at first, chewing on ice, too mean to answer. "Hambert's dog."

Til laughed loudly. It was a laugh that started out deep and booming, a head-turning laugh that ranged to a child's high giggle, a laugh that spread smiles like seeds, sowing new laughter all around it. Even Deputy Willis had to grin, his tired face wrinkling upward.

"What's so goddamn funny?" Mean Henderson never laughed. "The bear came at Hambert, too. He shot 'im with a shotgun right in the head. Bear *still* came after him, but he got inside his trailer just in time."

Til's laugh bubbled away inside his chest and ended in a moan. "Bullshit. Hambert's dog bit more people than that bear ever did. The idiot used to sic his dog on bears down by the dump just for fun."

"Seen any bear sign around the lodge?" The deputy was only half interested.

Til shook his head. "Nope."

Henderson frowned at him, still angry for being laughed at. "I'd like to see you laugh if that bear came at *you* out of the dark."

Til leaned into mean Henderson's anger, not away, and he smiled with a challenge in his smile, and he sang. "One day as Fiddlin' Dan went out to play, he met a grizzly standin' in his way." He slapped the countertop in time with his tune. "He

GERALD DI PEGO

24

couldn't climb a tree. He had no gun. He couldn't fly away. He was scairt to run."

Henderson looked meaner still. Deputy Willis grinned. Emma laughed aloud, and Til slid off his stool and danced. "Said the bear with a roar as he shook a mighty paw, you're Fiddlin' Dan from Arkansas . . ."

He hooked his arm into Henderson's as if to dance with him. Mean Winston pulled away and slapped at Til's arm, but Til was too fast, dancing away, singing. "I will leave you alone if you fiddle me a tune and organize a dance by the light of the moon."

He stopped beside Susan. Henderson called to him across the room.

"You're crazier 'n hell, Sharkis."

Susan turned to him. He saw her eyes were guarded. He saw no humor there, but he asked her anyway.

"Dance with me?"

She made a hard, don't-be-silly face and moved away to set a table. He turned to the register to pay for his lunch.

Kicking and shuffling down Lakeview Way, Til thought about how much he liked unpaved roads where he could feel dirt under his shoes, raise dust and kick stones and make a difference by his passing there. Paved streets barely noticed. Highways never even felt his step.

He also thought about the Widow Rendon and the empty place she had made inside of him last night. It had not been filled in the Clover Coffee Shop. Gloria would fill it, if she were home, if her window were open.

He kicked and shuffled and then trotted down Lakeview

FOREST THINGS

Way toward Gloria's window. Closed, it would mean that Chet was there or coming soon or neighbors were visiting. Open, ahh, open, it would mean come in. Now. Up the stairs. Into the room. Into the bed. She was there, already there, already naked and waiting.

Closed. He didn't even slow his step, just glanced at that side window and made sure again. Closed. Inside he felt empty and heavy at the same time. Her car was there. She was home. She was in there—warm, full, happy woman. She was home, but the window was closed, closing him out. Gloria, goddamnit, I need to be in there with you. Maybe later. He would go to the store and come back this way. Maybe then. He imagined her wide, soft smile and he felt her flesh with his hands, felt every part of her as he trotted down the unpaved road to her husband's store.

Chester Tumio sat in the center of a large metal building that was piled high with old desks, used mattresses, appliances of every kind, fifty tables and a hundred chairs. The daylight from the great wide door did not penetrate to the repair shop area where Tumio sat in the light of a used lamp, tacking a new vinyl cover on a secondhand chair. His work was slow, steady and totally absorbing. He never noticed Til until he spoke.

"Chet."

"Jesus! Holy . . . For God's . . . Christ!"

Til's laugh boomed and echoed as Chester hopped about. He was a small man, thick and muscular, doing a startled dance as Til's voice climbed to a giggle. Now Chet laughed too, swearing and punching Til's shoulder.

GERALD DI PEGO

26

"Ya son of a bitch! Creepin' up like . . . Scared the . . ."

Their laughter mingled and jangled off the metal walls, bounced between stacks of scarred furniture, reached even the shadowy places where dust lay thirty years deep.

"Could've gave me a heart attack."

"Didn't mean to."

"Turning into a goddamn Indian."

"How's the store going?"

"Fuck the store. I'm half dead from fear here. My hair probably turned white."

"It all fell out."

"I need some help here." He was reaching under a workbench and coming up with a pint of whiskey. "I need some attention." He took a pull on the bottle, wiped the top with his hand and passed it to Til. Til was still smiling, shaking his head. He took a drink and Chester watched him.

"Christ, you look like 'im."

"Who?"

"Who do you think?"

"My father?"

Chet straddled a stool at the workbench. Til hopped up on a table and sat with his legs dangling.

"With that beard—short like he wore it."

Til fingered his beard.

"Got the same wide back. Different face, I guess."

"I was thinking about my father. Last night."

"How old are you?"

"Thirty-one."

"Jesus, Til, that's older than *he* was."

"When?"

"When he left. He was thirty."

"Is that all he was?"

"Sure. I was . . . twenty-seven. He was thirty. Damn him for leavin' you like that, and bless his soul wherever he may be." Chet took a long drink from the bottle.

"I've got a feeling about where he is, Chet."

"Me too."

Til shook his head. "Not Japan."

"He always talked about it."

"Not Japan."

"Where do *you* think he is?"

"Everywhere."

"Serious, I mean."

"I mean it, Chet. He was going to Canada, remember? Talked about it for what? A year? Then his mind went on to Alaska. I remember people saying, 'When you goin' to Canada, Lex?' He'd say, 'Ah, to hell with Canada. Alaska's the place.' Just when he got people excited about Alaska, he got bored with it, and his mind went on to Japan."

"Like I said."

"Don't you see? No place was good enough. He was moving too fast."

Chet was silent, staring at memories, shaking his head at them. "He never went anyplace until the day he ran away. Never got further than Utica before that, maybe Syracuse once. Then he takes off for God knows where . . ."

"Where *could* a man like him go except everywhere?"

"Can't go everywhere."

"Yes. Everywhere at once."

"I mean serious, damn it, Til."

"The wind can."

"What?"

Chet offered the bottle. Til shook his head. Chet capped it and sagged on the stool, sighing. "If I'd been married then, I could've taken you in. Would've raised you as my own."

Til leaned back, studying the man, smiling. "Daddy. Daddy-Chet."

"Fuck you, Sharkis."

Their laughter echoed briefly once more. Then Til was serious.

"I ran last night. In the dark."

"Ran?"

"I didn't fall."

GERALD DI PEGO
———
28

"Ran where?"

"Ran down the mountain. Like I used to run with him. But never so fast before. And at night."

"Break your neck."

"Chet, I didn't fall."

"Good."

He wasn't getting through. "Don't you remember my dad running?"

"Running right out of this county. Leaving a ten-year-old boy, leaving a business with a partner that hardly knew how to run it. Leaving debts. I was in debt for eight years. His son shipped off to Utica. I remember him running."

"Don't you remember how he was in the forest, how he loved it?"

"Spendin' all his time building that cabin."

"He would run, Chet, remember?"

"Run where?"

"Through the forest with me! Jesus!"

They were silent while, above them, Til's echo rang against the metal ceiling and then faded and died.

"What're you gettin' so mad for? I can't remember everything."

"I'm not mad. It's just . . . Christ, don't forget 'im, okay? You knew him better than anybody. If you forget . . ."

"Twenty-one years ago he disappears . . ."

"Just try and remember the running."

Chet stared off, unfocused. He leaned on the workbench and drummed his strong blunt fingers there.

"He was like a damn Indian, too."

"And he would run, Chet. I'd follow him."

"And that day he just kep' runnin', and you came to me cryin'. You said . . ."

"Before that! Before that. There were times when we'd run so fast. I swear . . . he wouldn't touch the ground at all."

"Wouldn't touch the ground?"

"No." Til leaned close. "He wouldn't. And, see . . . I

FOREST THINGS

thought all that time he was *chasing* the wind. But last night . . ."

"Wouldn't touch the fuckin' ground?!"

"Aw, Chet . . ."

"Jesus Christ, what in God's name . . . have another drink, for Christ's sake. Don't go crazy on me. Here."

"I don't want a drink."

"Hey, where you goin'?"

"Back to the lodge."

"Stay awhile."

"No, I really have to get the boat and get back there." But he didn't move, standing ten feet from Tumio now, with lamplight and shadow between them, a space that would always be there, Til knew, because Chet didn't remember, or he had never known.

"Well," Chet slid off the stool, "at least stop by and see Gloria."

"I might. So long. Be well."

"You too. Wait."

Til turned. They stared a moment, and Chet said, "I'm sorry I don't remember."

"It's not your fault." Then Til smiled, and that snapped the cord of tension between them. Their bodies loosened, eyes flashed with humor and affection. "It's okay."

Open. Gloria's window was smiling at him, speaking to him. In. Come in. He wanted to dive through it. He angled through the wooded yard, passed the window and thought about it—two running steps then a headlong dive would send him through. But he didn't remember what furniture was there. He might break a table, break his neck. He almost did it. He felt the window tug at him as he passed. He trotted around to the back door, opened it and went in, hurrying to the living room to find that open side window. A sofa was there, that's all. He could have done it, should have. But it didn't matter. He was in, running up the stairs, unbuttoning his shirt, unbuckling his belt. Gloria.

"Honey?"

"You bet."

He stood in her doorway, peeling away clothes, dropping boots, grinning so hard his face hurt.

She was sitting up in bed, the sheet sliding down into her lap, her body naked, her hair mussed, her arms, legs and smile going wide, getting ready.

He ran and jumped on the bed and ran on the bed, shaking laughter from her. He knelt between her legs and they embraced, flesh on flesh. He almost wept.

He slowly fell back, pulling her with him, pulling her over him like a soft quilt. He closed his eyes. He ran his fingertips down her bare back and up the curve of her ass and down again and up again, lightly and more and more slowly. He felt her breasts crush against him, felt her long hair piling on his neck and chin, felt his own body loosen and sink into the mattress. Oh God, he had a sweet hour ahead of him. He was in Gloria's room, and Gloria was his blanket.

Til Sharkis was her bed, a narrow, bumpy bed, but warm and safe. She could never fall off. She rolled to the side to test her bed, and it caught her, steadied her with a strong hand on her ass, the fingers pressing deep and pinching just for fun. She put her head down on the hairy

FOREST THINGS

31

chest and rubbed the rib bones like harp strings. The bed shook with laughter. It was a magical, moving bed with hands that pulled gently at her hair to lift her face and gently put it down again, lips on lips, for a long, soft kiss; a bed with legs that moved against her own, sliding up, sliding down, running in slow motion.

They made love and didn't speak for half an hour.

       "See Chet?"
       "Yes."
       "He's sick."
"Didn't say."
"His headaches."
"Seemed all right."
She had arranged the bed for talking. They lay on the pillows, side by side, his arms around her. He hadn't wanted to move. He didn't want to talk. Even now his hand was sliding down her shoulder and fingering the top of her breast. Gloria was a wonderfully soft, fleshy woman, not quite plump. His fingers walked down to her nipple and danced upon it.

"Sharkis."
"Mm."
"Am I old?"
"No."
"I'm forty."
"Not old."
"Chet's gettin' so old. Sometimes, when he's tired, he looks sixty. He forgets things."
"I know."

GERALD DI PEGO
———

She was not aroused by the tiny dancer on her breast. Her look was far off and solemn.

"Does it bother you to talk about him?"

He placed his head against hers and shook it, no. They always talked about Chet. He was there with them, even though this was Gloria's bedroom and Chet had his own, even though he was one mile away, totally absorbed in the recovering of a chair or the slow sanding of an old desk, his small, careful hands powdered white with dust. His presence was there and had to be acknowledged.

"He's a good man."

Til's head nodded, yes, against hers.

"I love him, y'know."

"Me too." There was guilt, of course, buried under the "reasons." He knew that Gloria would now list the reasons.

"But, Sharkis, people need to play. I swear, Chet never played, ever. Chet must've been a serious little boy who built things, I swear. Lord . . . a sad little boy. He almost never touches me, y'know. Sleeping in his own room . . . I truly love 'im. You know that."

"I know." There was fear too, though Chet never, ever came home during the day. There was a low-burning fear, a pilot light. Til was sure Gloria must imagine it too—the scene of Chet opening the door, surprising them, surprising himself even more, his mouth and eyes stretching impossibly wide but not wide enough to take in the scene occurring before him.

"People need to play."

"I'll play with you."

"You say that, but you hardly come to town anymore. Aren't you tired of that lodge and that half-a-cabin you live in?"

"I fixed it up."

"It still rains inside, doesn't it?"

"Only when it rains outside."

"I'm serious. You should move to town. Get steady work."

"At Henderson's?"

FOREST THINGS

"Why not? You could still have your cabin. Lord . . . you're turnin' into another Egon. Look at you—with a beard, wild eye . . ."

"Egon—he's quite a man."

"He's an old fool with animals and bugs for company, burrs in his hair, rags for clothes. Is that going to be you? You're not a kid, y'know."

"For God's sake!"

"Well, you're not. None of us are. We have to think."

"I think."

"About what?"

"I think I want to play again." He laid her down in his lap, leaning over to kiss her eyes closed, but they wouldn't stay. She felt his organ stiffen against her back.

"Sharkis, that's not thinking. Not in the long term. We have to think in the long term."

"Don't you want to play?" He kissed her again and ran a hand down her hip and between her thighs.

"Will you get a job in town?"

He sat her up.

"Will you?"

He rose from the bed and began to dress.

"You won't, will you."

"Been here. Lived in town already."

"Sharkis, I'm talking about growing up, getting a job and making a *home*."

"Got a home."

"You don't even own it. You don't *own* that piece of a cabin."

"There's nothing here I want to own."

"You just want to be able to pick up and run like your father did."

His neck bulged and stiffened. His muscles were tight as he punched his arms through the sleeves of his shirt, and his eyes were not on her.

She was sorry she had said it. "Til . . ."

GERALD DI PEGO

"Seems to me he owned some things. Seems to me he had a child and a house in town and a business, too."

"Til, I didn't mean to . . ."

"Seems to me he had friends and women to play with, taxes to pay. He was a grown-up, wouldn't you say?"

"Please, not so loud."

"Wouldn't you say!"

She shouted in a whisper. "Til, please!"

"I *want* to live on that mountain. I feel good there. I know it better than he ever did and almost as good as Egon Webb knows it. I like it there. *That's* what holds me."

She began to cry. "Shhh. Please."

He lunged at her, and she gasped. He held her shoulders and lifted her partly off the bed. She thought he might shake her until she broke, but he kissed her instead, hard, on the forehead.

"I like coming to see you, Gloria. If you want me here just open your window. If you don't, leave it closed." He lowered her to the bed and kissed her mouth even harder, with love and anger, and he left.

The Chase family was up early and out to shoot. They stepped single file through a forest still wet and chilled and new, still unaware, Lyn thought, and her eyes swept off the path, eager to glimpse the forest things before they scattered and hid.

Mr. Chase carried his bow and three fierce, steel-tipped target arrows. Allan wore a .22 revolver in a holster at his side. Mrs. Chase walked behind her son and Lyn followed. The women were unarmed.

FOREST THINGS

"See that split trunk? Look straight. See where I'm pointing?" Chase pointed with one of his arrows, and his family followed the shaft, found the split birch. When all of their eyes struck the tree, the plant quivered, its sap oozing more quickly, its leaves trembling faster than the wind.

"You shoot for the left trunk. That's *your* left," Chase said. "I'll take the right." He fitted an arrow to his string. Allan drew the revolver. Mrs. Chase put her hands to her ears.

"We'll wake everybody up," Lyn said.

Chase frowned, testing the pull of his bow. "Mrs. Rendon's up. I saw her."

"I mean the whole forest."

Chase laughed without humor. Allan smiled, but it was a tight, pale look. He was nervous, afraid of missing.

"Draw your bead."

Arrow tip and revolver barrel rose up and slowly lowered. Animals hugged the ground and filled their lungs. Trees made themselves as thin as possible. The split birch shivered and tried to shrink.

"Fire."

Arrow whispered and bullet cracked. The .22 went between the trunks and snipped off the tip of a young pine, chipped some bark off a tough, old butternut and came to ground— but that arrow, that sharp, angry arrow drove into the right trunk, plunged through bark, through old wood and new wood, stabbed into the very center of the birch. A scream of shock pulsed out to the tip of every leaf and root. Sap bubbled out of the wound. The tree was still.

"Good shot, Dad."

"What about yours?"

Allan shrugged, wearing a false, twisted grin and eyes full of shame. Lyn had seen that look a thousand times, ever since Allan was two or three, ever since she could remember. It made her chest tighten and her throat fill with tears of pity and anger. She turned away.

"Give me." Chase reached out, and Allan put the revolver

GERALD DI PEGO

in his father's hand. Chase aimed at the split birch. "It's an easy shot, Al. Got a good three-inch margin around the center. How much could you shake?" Allan shrugged again, his smile more stretched and pained. Chase handed him the gun. "Try again."

Mrs. Chase came to stand beside her son, her hands pressed to her ears again. Lyn walked away. Allan held the revolver with both hands, fired.

Animals who had ventured out of shelter panicked and scattered. A chipmunk ran across Lyn's bare foot. She knelt down quickly and watched the animal disappear by standing still against the browns of wet earth and wood and old needles. Her eyes lost him, found him being a statue.

"Got it." Allan had hit the trunk.

"Good."

"Lyn, come here and try it."

"Don't want to." Her voice gave life to the statue. It ran away in little leaps and soft footfalls like the ticking of clocks.

"You try," Chase said to his wife.

"Oh, I hate the noise."

"Try the bow then."

Patti Chase reached for the taut bow as if it might spring to life in her hands. Chase helped her fit the arrow. He guided her from behind as she pulled.

"Keep it straight. Look at the target. Up a little. Fine. Shoot."

She drew back another inch before shooting, involuntarily raising the bow, sending the arrow off in a high arc that missed the birch and reached far into the forest. They didn't see or hear it land. Instead, they heard a scream, a man's scream.

Lyn kneeling in the path; Allan with the revolver a dead weight in his hand, his mouth open; Patti gripping the bow, holding her breath; Chase with his eyes straining to follow the arrow—they were a family of white stones.

The silence stretched long and thin but did not break. Then

FOREST THINGS

37

Patti's breath came in a whimper. Chase stepped forward, following the path of the arrow. Lyn rose from her knees like a dancer in a hushed and solemn passage, turning slowly to trade a wild stare with her brother, a look of fear with a seed of excitement in it—something has happened. Something has really happened now.

She went to her mother, who was holding a hand to her mouth, letting the bow slip from her fingers. It fell. Allan picked it up.

"Ouch."

They all turned exactly together, even Chase, already ten steps away. Their eyes ransacked the forest. Their ears ached for another sound.

Footsteps. A man came out of the shadows. Til Sharkis. The arrow was stuck in the front of his belt.

"This yours?"

They could tell from his walk, from his loose stance before them, hands on hips, that the arrow had not struck him. He had placed it there. No one was hurt. Their brains shouted the message. No one was hurt. Their bodies began to hear, began to breathe.

Allan laughed nervously, saying, "Oh, Jesus," again and again. Patti put both hands to her face, felt tears there. Lyn's eyes locked with Til's. He winked.

Chase was striding angrily across the clearing. Til met him halfway, the arrow bobbing before him, until only the shaft separated the two men.

"Mornin'," Till said. There was more than humor in his look. There was some anger there, some challenge.

For a moment it seemed that Chase's jaw was set so tight he couldn't speak, but his lips drew back from his teeth and he snapped, "What the hell do you think you're doing? Why did you scare us like that?"

"Scared me, too."

"Why did you scream?"

"Near miss."

GERALD DI PEGO

38

"I thought I killed someone," Patti said, smiling through tears, and Allan said once more, "Oh, Jesus."

"It's no joke," Chase said.

"Darn right." Til took the bow from Allan, hefted it. "Bullets and arrows whizzing around me. I thought the Indians wanted their forest back."

Allan laughed a one-note laugh, an outburst of nervous relief. Chase turned on the boy and took his arm. "You think it's funny?"

Til saw those strong fingers curl around the boy's upper arm.

"No, Dad."

He saw shame wash into the boy's eyes, and he looked away. Lyn was watching him. He turned to point the arrow shaft at her.

"Here's your arrow."

She hesitated, then put a hand on it. It was stuck in one of his belt holes. She pulled and he stumbled toward her, staring at her. Chase came between them and yanked the arrow free.

"I'll show you some cliffs you can shoot against," Til said. "About a fifteen-minute walk. That way, nothing gets hurt."

"Don't worry about it," Chase said.

"Oh, I'm finished anyway.'" Patti waved a hand at all of them and walked to the path. "I'm going back. I never should have tried to . . . I'm really . . ."

"Before you go—" Til's words stopped her in midstride. Her head turned back, but her body was still leaning forward, rushing home. "I'm going to town later to pick up another couple—guests for cabin B. I'll have room in the boat for one, if somebody wants to come."

Patti shrugged and looked at Chase.

"Yes," Lyn said.

"No," Chase said.

Lyn looked away, at no one, at the forest. In a moment she followed her mother down the path to the cabin.

Til turned to the boy. "Allan?"

"Uh . . . yeah." He said it with a question on his face, turning to his dad. Chase just moved away, taking the bow from Til.

"About an hour," Til said. "See you at the boat."

Til was gassing the outboard. The Widow came out of the house and walked toward the small pier. Til watched her angling toward him, fixing things, righting things as she came, righting an overturned bucket, tossing a fallen log on the woodpile, snatching up a piece of paper from the yard, keeping things in their natural places. She did it with her eyes, too, glancing at the flowers as she passed, her eyes saying, "Bloom"; glancing at the sky—"Don't cloud"; at the mountain—"Stay there." She was the keeper of the lodge and the world that surrounded the lodge, and she liked things clean, ordered and in place. She stood above him on the pier.

"Spending an awful lot of time in that cabin of yours."

He went on working in the boat. "Just my own time."

"Catch your death sleeping up there."

"I've got it just about windproof now."

"Been so cold at night."

He glanced up at her, but she was looking out across the water, her eyes magnets again, drawing the blue from lake and sky, leaving them pale. "You sleep better when it's cold, don't you?"

Her eyes blazed with a tight blue flame like a blowtorch. He readied for it, but she didn't turn to him. He finished with the motor.

"I'm taking the Chase boy with me."

GERALD DI PEGO

40

"You going to have room coming back with the new people and their luggage?"

"Mm, forgot about the luggage."

"Better leave 'im."

Til considered it, his look wandering to the Chases' cabin where the door was opening and Allan was coming out, letting the door snap closed behind him, walking toward Til and pretending not to look at him.

"I'll take him," Til said. "We'll make it fit."

"Suit yourself. Just don't let anybody or anything get wet. People love to sue nowadays."

She moved off. Til waved Allan into the boat. "Untie us first. That's it. Jump in."

Til started the motor and turned the boat slowly away from the pier. Allan got settled in the bow seat, facing him. Til smiled at the boy and throttled the engine to full. Allan's smile had to fight its way out. It came, a small, secret thing he tried to hide, but then the bow bounced on the waves and the wind framed his face with his wild, dancing hair, and the smile broke loose and jumped into his eyes.

Halfway across, Til killed the motor.

"What's wrong?"

"Nothin'. Can't stand the noise for too long." They drifted, turning, their own wake rapping at the side of the boat.

Allan looked about, trying to hide his concern as he floated halfway from anywhere with a man he didn't know.

"Relax."

"I'm relaxed."

Til stretched his legs, put his feet up on the next seat, leaned back on his elbows. "Great lookin' day." Allan nodded. "Warm when the wind stops." The boy nodded again. "Why don't you take your shirt off?"

"I'm okay."

"Take it off."

"Why?" The boy was looking pale, his mouth turning down a bit with fear.

FOREST THINGS

Til smiled. "Just slip it off a minute, Allan. I want to see your arm."

"My arm? Why?"

"Please."

"No."

"I want to see your arm where your father grabbed you. Please."

Allan touched his arm, remembering. "It's okay," he said, but he began unbuttoning the shirt. He slipped it down his arm and stared at the bruise, at the new bruise on top of old bruises, at the faint purple outline of fingers. "It's okay."

Til looked at the mark and wanted to touch it gently, wanted to hold Allan's head in his hands and make the boy look at him, and tell the boy something that would help. He wanted to smooth the wind-crazed hair around that long, joyless face. He wanted to hug the boy and hug his sister, too, and lightly kiss the bruise that marked *her* arm, and he wanted to take the mother's hand and squeeze it, for she probably wore her own armband—the family crest.

"Doesn't hurt," Allan said, pulling up the shirt. "Why did you want to see it?"

Til shrugged. "Curious." But Allan stared at him, waiting for more. "My father never hurt me," Til said.

"I said it didn't hurt." There was shame again in the boy's eyes. "My dad got's a temper, and he's strong. He's okay."

"Want to come out here and fish sometime?"

"He just . . . what?" Allan slowly shifted subjects in his mind. Images of his father were eased out by a big fish exploding out of the lake, showering diamonds, flapping a silver tail in the sky, a magic fish connected to Allan by a taut line and a pole that quivered with desperate life. He liked the picture. He began to nod. "I guess so. Sure. Must be great fishing."

"No, but it's peaceful." Til grinned and watched the boy turn away, hiding that secret smile.

Allan stretched his legs and put his feet up on the next seat, leaned back on his elbows.

They drifted, eyes closed to the sun.

GERALD DI PEGO

42

"Well, lookit Sharkis."

"Who's your friend?"

"Back so soon?"

"Got a helper there, huh?"

"Take a load off."

When Emma brought their Cokes, she leaned close to Allan and winked. "What're you learnin' from Mr. Sharkis here?"

The boy shrugged. Emma's dirty laugh whispered through her teeth. She turned to Til. "What're you teachin' him, hah? Say . . ." Then closer, softer, dirtier. "Susan's here today."

She laughed again and moved to her grill by steps and twitches. Allan looked at Til, and Til gave a shrug, then he quietly imitated Emma's laugh. Allan hid a smile under his hand.

"Get a call for us yet, Dan?" Til said. "We've got a couple of guests supposed to be here or call by noon."

"S'only eleven."

"Get any calls, Dan?"

"No calls. What's the name?"

Til checked a piece of paper in his wallet. "Dermitter."

"Dermitter?" Emma frowned over her grill. "What kind of name is that?"

"Last name," Til said.

Allan laughed a small laugh—but at the wrong time, sending Coca-Cola up into his nose the back way, bringing on coughing, tears, back-pounding from Til and a chorus of concern.

"What's the matter with the boy?"

FOREST THINGS

43

"Give 'im water."

"Let 'im breathe."

"Stand 'im up."

"What's the matter with the boy?"

They ate cheeseburgers and pie. Allan caught Til watching Susan, and he watched too, and Til watched Allan.

"Like her looks?" Til said.

"Hm? She's okay."

"Watch her eyes." Then, louder. "Susan . . . Hi."

"Hi." She didn't look at him.

"How you doing?"

"All right." Her eyes brushed over them, looking bored, straining for blasé. She walked into the kitchen.

"See?" Til said.

"What?"

"You find any place in her eyes, any space?"

"Space?"

"Room. Room for you to fit in?"

Allan stared a moment. "She seemed snotty."

"That's exactly what I'm saying. You're smart, Allan. You're an eye reader. Finish up. We'll take a walk."

They walked by mean Henderson's place.

"I don't know if that's Sharkis I see or old Egon."

That stopped Til, not because it was mean, he expected meanness from Henderson and was disappointed if it didn't come, if the man was too busy or not feeling well. It stopped him because of what Gloria had said—that he was turning into another Egon Webb, a fool, she said.

"Started talkin' to yourself yet, Sharkis?"

GERALD DI PEGO

"See that battered up '70 Chevy over there, Allan—leaking oil, needs paint? Look close. That's really a man named Winston. Honk for the boy, Winston."

"Crazier than a loon."

"Hear that, Allan? Hey, Winston, you still loaded for bear?"

"We're gonna get that animal," Henderson said. "He raided a camp last night."

"Stole somebody's potato chips, did he? How do you know it was him?"

"Big tracks."

Til smiled and shook his head. "Just can't wait to shoot your gun off, can you. It's loaded and cocked and just lying there in your gun rack and you touch it and pick it up and it's oiled and ready and it seems like it'll just burst if it doesn't go off soon, right? You just gotta shoot something or die!"

"There was a big bear by our place," Allan said.

"When?" Henderson was frowning with concentration, down to business.

"About . . . four days ago."

"A tiger," Til said. "The kid can't tell the difference. Come on, Allan."

"You see that bear?"

"No," Allan said. "But I heard it. Remember?"

But Til was already jogging away, and the boy followed. They ran across the road and down to the lakeshore. The bathers' beach was half a mile north. Here it was driftwood and boulders, old logs and smooth stones.

Allan sidearmed a flat stone, spinning it so that is struck the water and grew legs, leaping another ten yards, touching, then taking another joyous bounce.

"Fly," Til said, and spun a stone that tipped an incoming ripple and soared upward, for an instant alive, for twenty feet a bird, then down again, a stone again.

"Pretty one." He tossed a flat rock to Allan. The boy caught it and looked at the swirls of white, veins of blue.

FOREST THINGS

"Fly it," Til said.

The boy gave it flight.

"The kid gets a three." Til picked a stone that curved and dove deep.

"Not even a one," Allan said.

"Smart-ass."

Allan's stone skipped five times.

"Show-off."

Til's sank again.

"Want me to show you how?" Allan said.

"Want to get wet?" He chased Allan for a moment, the boy running around boulders and jumping over logs, fighting to hold back the smile that struggled and twisted and came out crooked.

They stopped, panting, and settled back into skipping stones—stones half in sand, centuries old, surf-washed and sun-dried a million times, stones until this day, until Allan Chase and Til Sharkis fingered them out of the sand and gave them life aloft.

"Why didn't you tell him about the bear?" Allan said. "It could be the one they want."

"It is."

"Then why?"

"He's a hunter—Winston. Champion hunter. The sheriff'll hire 'im to kill that bear."

"So? He raided a camp."

"Not supposed to keep food in camp. Supposed to hang it on a tree away from camp. The bear is just a scrounger. There—a four."

Allan threw a six. "My dad's a hunter, but he still loves animals."

"He does?" Til was surprised.

"Yes, he does. Doesn't your dad hunt?"

Til drew back and flung a flat black stone, sent it speeding along just above the water, then it touched and suddenly curved upward into the sky and vanished.

GERALD DI PEGO

46

"Where'd it hit?" Allan said. "How many skips?"

Til stared at the sky that had closed tight around that black stone. "Gone," he said.

His face began to change, the muscles slackening, jaw dropping a bit, the eyes no longer searching the sky. His eyes were back twenty-one years, searching the forest for his father. His face was a child's face, even now—behind the beard, beneath the lines. He was ten and searching and sending his voice out among the trees until it was gone, and he could only scream in a whisper and cry without a sound. He was ten and as alone as anyone could possibly be—mother unknown to him, father now lost, day gone to darkness. Still he screamed in a broken whisper. Dad!

The Memory was on him, stuck fast, its claws dug deep. It was heavy, and it was hurting him. He turned to Allan and looked at a stranger. He turned to the road and followed it with his mind to Gloria's home, to her window, to her bed.

"Allan?" The boy was throwing stones again. "You okay here for a while?"

"Why?"

"I need half an hour, forty minutes. I want to see a friend. I'll be right back. Will you be okay?"

"What if those people come?"

"They're not even due for half an hour. Just tell 'em I'll be right back. Okay?"

"Sure," Allan said, and he watched Til wave and turn and take a skipping step, a short hop that was like the shifting of gears, easing him into a trot down the gravel road. He watched Til's run, admiring the grace of it, and when the man was out of sight, Allan still listened to his gritty footsteps diminishing in rhythm like an echo until actual sound blended with the memory of sound, and he couldn't tell if he were really hearing Til or not. He wished for a space in the trees so he could see him once more. He wished he were the friend Til was running to see.

FOREST THINGS

47

Chester Tumio checked again to make sure there were no customers in or near the building. He walked once more out of the dark shop, squinting against the sunlight, watching for possible customers approaching on the road. He turned and began searching through a stack of dusty, rusted signs near the door, flat metal rectangles bound together in common decay. He pulled them apart. *Sold. Yes, we're open! Squirt. Be back in ____ minutes.* He closed the door and hung the *Be back in ____ minutes* sign on it, studying the blank space between *in* and *minutes*. He decided to leave it blank. He searched again for the faintest possibility of a customer and saw no one. He stood still for a time, unable to move, held by the gravity of that big, squat, silent building behind him.

He suddenly stepped away from it, out of its reach. Chet Tumio was leaving his store to go home, leaving in the middle of the day for the first time in five years.

As he walked to his house, he tried to form the sentences he would need. "Gloria, you know what? You know what I've been thinking? Gloria . . . ?" It had begun early in the morning when Sy Henning had brought in the old cabinet. Maybe he should start by telling her about the cabinet. "Henning brought in a cherrywood cabinet, old thing. Japanese. Really fine work. Those carvings the Japs do. Really . . . It started me thinking. You know how I always talk about . . ." He erased that, realizing he hadn't spoken to her about Japan in years. "I was always talking about Japan, remember? About how my partner, Sharkis, loved the place and probably went there

GERALD DI PEGO
———
48

when he ran off and left Til? Remember?" She wouldn't. "Anyway, I saw the cabinet, and I remembered. I remembered that it was *me* that started the whole thing about Japan. *I* always wanted to go there, and *I* read a book on it. I told Sharkis and he got it from *me*. Japan. I used to get so mad thinking about him enjoying Japan and me left with his debts. So I saw the cabinet, and I said to Henning, 'I'm going there.' He didn't believe me, but after he left, I said it again, out loud. 'I'm going there.' And I am. We *are*, Gloria."

He wondered if he could handle all that. He wondered if it made sense. He was at the back door of his house now and wondering if he were crazy. Going away. Closing the store. Japan.

He entered quietly and stood in the empty, humming kitchen, rehearsing. "Gloria, we're going on a trip." He didn't hear her. He knew she napped during the day. He walked into the living room and looked at the stairway. He closed his eyes to get it right, saying the words in his mind. "I've been thinking about Japan, Gloria." She would just stare. He imagined her staring. He sat on the sofa to think it out once more before he went up there and woke her and gave her the news. "Gloria, there's someplace I want to go." She would think Utica or at the most, Buffalo. "Why should Sharkis—"

He was in the middle of a silent sentence when it happened —the strangest thing that had ever happened to Chester Tumio. There was nothing in his mind, no reason, no handle, nothing to help him believe what he saw. He could only stare —with his mouth open and his breath sucked in—and wonder as Til Sharkis came flying into the room through an open window, landed beside him on the sofa and somersaulted to the floor with a great crash.

FOREST THINGS

49

Til's landing set lamps tinkling and knickknacks rocking on their shelves. The floor shook under him and the heating ducts rang from basement to roof. He sat still, feeling that the house would fall down around him, hoping it would.

It didn't, so he had to turn, slowly turn his head toward Chet and face the man. Tumio was suspended in time. All movement, breathing, thinking, had stopped two seconds ago. Looking at Chet was like looking back in time. He was a photograph. He was a record of a moment in the past. The man was leaning away from Til at a steep angle, hands gripping knees, his face white with shock and disbelief, his eyes and mouth stretched wide but not wide enough to take in the scene occurring before him.

Til rejected every word, every possible greeting or explanation that rushed into his mind. He said nothing. He smiled a strange, weak smile.

Gloria came halfway down the stairs and stopped, staring at the two of them. The men turned together to look at her. No one spoke until Chet said in a whisper of great wonder, "I was just thinkin' about his dad."

His voice shook the moment loose, started the clocks ticking again. They were back in the present. Gloria shouted, "What happened!?"

"Til came in the window. I was just thinking about his dad, and in he came. Flying!"

Til shrugged. Gloria sat down on the stairs and said, "Oh, dear Lord." "Flying," Chet said again, and Til suddenly felt his stomach and chest grow tight. Inside was a great bubble of mad laughter that he didn't dare let out.

Chet was babbling, excited. "He flew in just as I was thinkin' his father's name, at that very second. Bam! In he came. I said to myself, 'Why should Sharkis—' and it was like I called him. I was about to say to myself, 'Why should Sharkis enjoy it and not me?' I was talkin' about Japan. You know, it was *me* who first thought about goin' there. Your father'd talk about it like *he'd* read the book, but it was really *me* that read it. I started it and I should've been the one to go, goddamnit, and now I am. Me and Gloria are goin' to Japan, and if I see your father, I'll tell him he's a son of a bitch for me, and what should I tell him for you?"

Til was silent, still waiting for the question and wondering what he would answer, but the question wasn't coming. Chester Tumio was not asking him why. Why? Why did you fly through my window? Instead he was talking about Til's father and about Japan. Japan.

Til got to his feet and glanced at Gloria. She had buried her face in her knees. He turned to Chet and felt that bubble of laughter rise into his throat. He swallowed it.

"Chet, he won't be in Japan. He never went there. You have a great time though."

Chet rose and offered Til a solemn handshake.

"Are we really going?" Gloria's voice was muffled in her lap.

"We're really goin' to Japan." Chet spoke with wonder at his own words. "We are."

Til walked to the door. "That's great. I have to go now. I left a friend at the beach so . . ." He smiled at them both. Laughter filled his mouth and pushed against his teeth, laughter not at Chet or Gloria, more at himself, at life, at people, crazy laughter that would topple him over and hurt his sides and never stop. He kept his mouth clamped shut against it. He waved and went out the door and down the steps and skipped into his loping trot.

FOREST THINGS

All the way to the beach, the laughter quivered in his chest. When Allan told him the Dermitters were stuck on the road with car trouble, he giggled. When he learned it was a flat tire and no jack, his eyes began to tear. When mean Henderson lent them a jack but refused to let them use his truck, Til chuckled and had to walk away fast.

He asked Dan Clover if they could use his pickup to take the jack to the Dermitters. They were only five miles out of town on the mountain highway. Clover said yes, and wanted to go along; so did two of his customers, Gil Coleman and Mel Fennis.

Til rode in the back of the truck, bouncing about with Allan and Fennis, and with every bounce the bubble threatened to burst inside of him. He wore a constant fool's smile, and his eyes were brimming with mindless humor. He was sure Allan thought he was insane, and that thought only made him want to laugh.

Michael Dermitter's car was crippled, leaning awkwardly on the drop-off side of the mountain highway.

It looked pitiful and helpless, and the sight of it filled him with anger. In the wounded Porsche, he saw his own

GERALD DI PEGO

pitifulness, helplessness, foolishness. The car was a sign leaning toward him, pointing at him: "This man doesn't know what he's doing."

He turned his back to it and watched his wife struggle up the steep cliffside above the road aiming toward a stand of pine.

"Careful," he said. She went on, smiling, enjoying the air and the silence and the scents, even the dust and sharp rocks, making sure with her smile that he *knew* she was enjoying herself, that everything was all right, that she didn't blame him for leaving the jack at home.

He hated her smile now because he was sure it was stuck on to make him feel better. It made him feel worse, more childish, foolish, not because he had forgotten the jack, but because he had forgotten the jack here, in this place where he was a stranger, in this land of few people who all knew each other and knew their own kind and looked with suspicion and a touch of scorn on newcomers like him, tourists who didn't fish or hunt or tie knots or use tools, men who dressed wrong and moved clumsily and made silly mistakes. He had wanted to somehow win their approval or at last ease into their world unnoticed. Instead he had made his entrance wearing clown makeup and rubber feet.

LOOK, said the blinking hazard lights of his car. HERE, said the tilt of the Porsche. LOOK HERE AT THIS FOOL.

He sat down in the dirt of the roadside and immediately checked around him for any movement. Here the ground was alive. He didn't like earth that moved on tiny legs and attacked with stingers and pinchers and burrowing heads and poisoned tails. He felt at ease on cement and carpeting. He felt in place in a courtroom, in his office, on a tennis court, in his apartment, even in his traitorous car.

"Honey . . . ?" His wife was moving at a dangerous angle fifteen feet above the road. "Not too far, okay?"

Mag slipped and dug her hands into the loose earth to catch herself. She popped a button on her shirt, broke a nail

FOREST THINGS

and laughed. When she laughed, her eyes, always alive, moving, seeming to vibrate with energy, danced.

"Are you all right?"

She ignored her husband and went on, scrambling and stretching and reaching the shade of three pine trees on a ledge of earth above the highway. She sat on a cushion of needles and breathed deeply, brushing a sleeve across her sweaty forehead and the hair that had fallen there.

"God, this is great." She didn't add "come up here" because she knew he wouldn't, and also she wanted to be alone in the shade that she had earned.

She gave one tree the soft palm of her hand and let the rough bark scrape it, hurt it. She leaned back against another and felt it catch her hair. She closed her eyes. The three giant pines were surrounding her, their roots pinching hard at her buttocks and thighs, their trunks catching and scratching her. They were closing in, reaching down. They would soon be tearing at her. She would laugh in joyous pain. They would take her clothes first, then her skin. They would wrap her in rough bark. Then there would be four pines on the ledge of earth above the highway, and down below her husband would be calling.

"Mag. Babes? I think they're here."

Til hopped out of the pickup and glanced at the wounded car and the worried man next to it. Dermitter was about Til's age, a little younger. He was not fat, but his skin seemed loose on his frame, giving him a round and slightly puffy baby face.

GERALD DI PEGO
———
54

Dan Clover, Gil Coleman, Fennis and Allan gathered around as Dermitter pointed into his empty trunk—the luggage was piled on the roadside—and explained how he had taken out the jack when packing, and forgot to put it back. The men stood with hands on hips, looking from the trunk to the flat tire, nodding in a solemn way that threatened to unlock the laughter inside of Til.

He turned away from them to see Mag Dermitter descending the mountain, streaks of dust and a landslide of pebbles following her to the road.

She smiled at him and the others and began slapping the dust from her jeans. Making smoke, Til thought. The woman is on fire—wild hair around a sweaty, open, darkly pretty face, with eyes that laughed and burned up energy, making smoke. He grinned at his urge to help slap the dust from her compact thighs and round, tight buttocks. He noticed the popped button on her shirt and the flesh of her breast and the bit of wispy blue bra. He blessed all such wispy things, blessed all breasts and the silky, delicate things that bound them. He sent a mental kiss to her open shirt and another to her forehead, saying hello.

"Hi, I'm Til Sharkis from the lodge."

The jack didn't work. Til sucked in his lips and bit them to hold back the mad laughter. The Porsche was levered up. It slipped and fell back down for the tenth time.

They organized the lifting of the small car by manpower. Til and Dermitter, Dan Clover, Gil Coleman and Fennis would raise it up, hold it while Mag slipped off the flat and Allan rolled the spare into place.

Clover counted. "One, two, three, lift!" Ten arms strained and lifted. The heavy metal rose. Rubber tires left the ground, the car moving faster than they had imagined, moving up and out of their hands. They reversed their grips quickly, trying to catch it, but it was turning over, revolving slowly and inevitably now, like a person asleep. It crashed down on its side.

They had heaved the Porsche all the way over, and the fact, the giant fact they all were witnessing and not believing, was that the car was not stopping. It was too close to the cliff, already over the edge, easing itself over again, banging down on rock and shrub and slowly revolving again, moving on, crashing, turning, over and over down the mountainside, grinding a great cloud of dust from the earth, while above it stood seven statues hewn in poses of surprise, stone arms half-lifted, mouths chiseled wide. One of the statues disappeared. Six were left watching as the Porsche, crumpled like paper now, stopped at a stand of trees two hundred feet down the mountain.

They became people again, hands of flesh moving to faces or coming to rest on hips, mouths closing, heads shaking. "Christ. Holy . . . Oh, shit. Son of a bitch!" Dermitter swore the loudest. "Son of a bitch!" Mag came beside him, staring at him, but he wouldn't turn away from the battered Porsche. "Son of a bitch!"

The others turned sorry, solemn eyes on each other, on Mag. Allan stood over the spare tire, his body still ready to roll it and fit it onto a wheel that wasn't there. He was pale, scared. None of them noticed that Til had left—until they heard the sound.

It was an animal, they thought, something big, something hurt and squealing. They all turned and looked toward the forest, saw nothing. The squealing faded, then came back and opened up into laughter, a man's wild, mad laughter.

GERALD DI PEGO

Til Sharkis was in there screaming and crying and moaning, a volcano of laughter, erupting, exploding, out of control.

They listened, and slowly came under the spell of that laughter—Allan first, walking away, tight inside, moving into the truck and lying down there, trying to muffle the laughter that came and brought him to tears. The Tilima city men were next, looking at each other, then trying not to look at each other, trying not to smile. They turned their struggling faces away, but Til's chuckling broke them down. They laughed in whispers first. They staggered away, stomachs hurting. The voice from the forest found them, forced it out of them—loud laughter that could not be caught and held.

Mag stared at her scowling husband, hoping to see a crack appear, looking for the faintest flash of humor in his eyes. The mad voice of the forest was already washing over her in great waves, each wave higher, stronger. She knew she would go under, surrender soon. She put her hands to her mouth. Laughter surged from Til, crested and broke. She could hear his long, tortured intake of breath. The voice came again, high notes. She sat down in the dirt and covered her face. She was soon shaking, aching under the spell. She looked up once more at Michael, found him staring at her, found that first hint of madness in his look. Good. So he was not immune, so they could all lose their minds together, give up minds and bodies to that laughing forest thing.

They laughed and subsided and laughed again. They quieted, moaning, began to try to speak, be reasonable again, behave responsibly again, but one would weaken and laugh, and they would all crumble and stagger about as though punched in the belly, taking weak, aimless steps in the road, leaning on the truck.

One by one, each of the Tilima men went to Michael Dermitter and put a hand on his head or thumped his shoulder, saying with a gesture, "You're okay. This man is all right." Michael had his acceptance, stronger, warmer than he could have hoped. Mag, too, was welcomed with rough hands on

FOREST THINGS

her back, but her eyes kept returning to the forest. She waited for Til. She wanted to study the magician who had worked the spell.

When Til came, he had left his laughter behind. He was drained, peaceful now, only his eyes awash with humor. She hoped to see him laugh, to put together that disembodied forest sound with this erect man, bearded, strong and graceful man. But he laughed no more, and when he helped her up into the truck and sat across from her, he didn't search her as before, didn't glance at her breasts and legs. He kept his black, black eyes full on her face and studied her as openly as she studied him.

The boat rode low in the water, packed with the Dermitters and their luggage, Allan and Til. Til stopped the engine halfway across the lake, and Michael asked what was wrong.

"It's the noise," Allan said. Til nodded and let the boat drift a bit, let the Dermitters see and hear and feel the Tilima country.

"Beautiful," Mag said, and her husband took her hand. They searched the lake, the shore, the mountains.

"That's the lodge and cabins dead ahead," Til said. "And halfway up the mountain behind them, above the white cliffs, where the trees are thick—that's my place."

"Imagine living here. And not even here, not in the resort, but halfway up the mountain. *Living* here."

Mag was unpacking, organizing, assigning a place to every sock and shirt and shoe. "Not even cars, not on the mountain. No TV of course, maybe not even a radio."

"And he probably can't read," Michael said. "What are you doing? Can't we just live out of the suitcases? Christ."

But she had a drawer, closet or cabinet for everything, even the camera, the keys, sunglasses, loose change, until everything had its place except them—the man seated on the couch with his feet on the table, the woman in the center of the room, half-turned, thinking, searching. "Imagine never leaving."

When she turned to Michael, he was picking up one corner of the curtain, looking out the window. She felt something catch inside of her, a spasm of fear, almost nausea. "It isn't there," she said. "I looked."

"What?" he didn't look away from the window.

"The park."

Now he turned, angry, hurt. "I heard something out there."

"I was just teasing."

He peered out again, and she looked over his shoulder. There was a light on over the back door of the lodge, a bare bulb, an intruder, foreign to the night, attacked by moths and beetles, encircled by a darkness that seemed to be advancing, slowly erasing the light on the lawn, the light in the air and on the building, leaving a smaller and smaller circle around the bulb. "There's nothing," she said. "Crickets."

"No, I heard something scratching around out there."

FOREST THINGS

She knelt on the couch beside him and looked out for a moment, then changed the focus of her eyes to look at the glass itself, at her husband's face reflected there, at his eyes. She felt afraid again, and ashamed.

In New York City their apartment looked out on a park, a small city park of scattered trees and benches and a playground. It was not lighted at night, but people would come there—street children out late, lovers, bums. Mag and Michael had watched them, absently at first, casually, drawn by an argument or the creak and thump of the seesaw. They had knelt on their bed to look out of the high bedroom windows, amused at first, giggling, whispering, but then Michael began to stay longer at the window. Often she would fall asleep with him still kneeling and watching, silent and serious now.

They used to go to bed at eleven, bringing their law briefs or magazines to read, but Michael began to get restless by ten or ten-thirty. He would go to bed early, turn out the light. She knew he was in there watching. When she came into the room, he would hear her coming and pretend to be asleep or almost asleep. But she knew. He was watching the dark park, watching it more and more.

Once she awoke in the middle of the night and saw him kneeling there. It was a long time before she moved. She didn't speak. She rose up beside him. He didn't turn to her. They watched together.

They saw three boys seated in the grass, passing a cigarette. They followed the red dot from fingers to lips, heard the muffled laughter. They remained silent, immobile, almost hypnotized by the moving red dot, by the actions of people unaware of them, by the feeling of invisibility. When the boys left, Mag began to lie down. "Wait," Michael said. He didn't turn from the window. She waited, watched. A couple came. They brought a blanket and spread it to lie down in the darkness, becoming only shapes, shadows darker than the grass. They soon came together to make one shadow, moving slowly, dancing prone. In a while Mag saw the man rise to his

GERALD DI PEGO

60

knees to take down his pants. She felt ashamed. Not because they were watching, but because they somehow needed to watch. She felt empty. Life was outside on the wet grass. They were behind the window, dry, almost dead, only watching.

She lay down and waited and hoped Michael would come to her. In a moment, he did. They made love, but she felt he was only half with her. She felt that above them, in the dark glass of the window, his reflected face remained trapped, staring out with eyes going dead.

She had decided then—she would never watch again. She would do. She would act. She would be the someone who was watched, studied by empty people who hid in dark rooms and only looked.

Tonight there was no park, nothing to watch but bugs around a bare bulb. "Let's go to bed. Come on." She pulled at the back of his belt. He let the curtain drop.

In bed, her body made sure he knew. She didn't want to talk. She wanted him, wanted him around her, on top of her, inside her. She wanted *them*, stuck together, one thing without thought, knowledge or past.

He was as desperate as she. They lunged at each other, trying to cross a gulf, close the distance, cover the ground that had come to separate them. The gap was exactly the size of a small city park, full of shadows. They could not reach each other. They held each other tightly, feeling nothing but their own desperation.

Mag drifted into fantasy. The bed beneath her grew hard and knobby with exposed roots, sharp with twigs. Loose earth and pine needles stuck to her sweat, covered her back. The

FOREST THINGS
———

forest moved around her, whipped and screaming, punished by the wind. On her was a forest creature, strong and wild, hands in her hair, teeth at her breast. She closed her eyes tighter and tighter until she saw him, his face, his beard, and his black, black eyes.

They had finished, or rather Michael had finished, and the lovemaking had stopped. He had rolled on his side, his face close to hers. Each wondered who would speak first and what would be said.

He whispered, "That was so nice. Was it good for you?"

"Yes."

"I wish . . ."

"What?"

He smiled. She heard it in his his words, an embarrassed smile. "I wish I could tell. I used to be able to tell. You used to . . . You'd respond more."

"I'm sorry."

"Remember?"

"I'm tired from today."

"You used to practically scream." He chuckled in a whisper, remembering.

She remembered too, and smiled. "You were afraid someone would call the cops."

They laughed together, but when they stopped, the silence lay heavily on the bed between their faces. Each hoped the other would speak.

He whispered, "You'd say, 'Oh my God!' "

"I remember."

"You'd practically scream it."

"I'm sorry."

"Don't be sorry. Just . . ."

"I'm sorry."

They touched lightly, drained of energy, approaching sleep. Then they both stopped breathing, opened their eyes, lay absolutely still. They had heard the beast.

It rubbed against their cabin, and the wall trembled. It

GERALD DI PEGO

coughed or growled, a sound from deep inside some massive body. It scratched at the ground.

"Jesus . . ."

"Shhh!"

She moved her legs over the side of the bed.

His whisper was sharp, hissing. "Where are you going?"

"To see what it is."

"Don't!"

She began walking slowly to the window but stopped. The beast was at the front porch now. Mag became a nude mime in the center of the room, head tilted in the position for listening, arms half up, fingers stretched out. She moved silently to the front door, her toes searching for objects in her path.

"Don't go to the door!"

Just as she touched the handle, the beast bumped into the wood railing of their porch, and the railing screamed and splintered.

"Jesus! Mag, come here!"

She slowly opened the door, just a crack, letting in one stripe of moonlight that streaked down her naked body and ran along the bed where Michael knelt.

"Mag!"

She saw nothing.

Til Sharkis awoke and rolled over on his back. The day was already up and washed and waiting outside his cabin. He stepped out of bed and went to the door, opened it and met a morning so fine it made him smile. The smile cracked his mask of sleep, and it fell from his face like shattered glass. His eyes blinked themselves clear.

FOREST THINGS

He took a long, deep breath, sucking in several clouds, leaving the sky clear blue from mountain to lake. He stretched his arms as wide as that sky and yawned so hard he shouted, and his shout became a song.

"Oh! Get along home, Cindy, Cindy. Get along home . . ."

His voice creaked and whistled as it awoke, refusing to sing, demanding to cough. He coaxed it toward the melody. Singing, he put on his underwear and his jeans, hopping about, one leg in, one out.

"I'll marry you some day!"

He sang and hopped, and his singing bounced against new walls, made by his own hands. His hopping shook the shelves he had built to hold the tools he had used to build the shelves.

"I wish I was a needle, as fine as I could sew!"

He jumped backward to land sitting on the bed and began to put on his boots. He had made the bed frame by hand and carried the mattress and spring up the mountain on his back.

Years ago, he and his father had slept rolled in blankets on the cabin's dirt floor. It was really only a lean-to then, with a stone fireplace that had always been there. His father had found the handmade hearth and fallen chimney and built the shelter around it. He thought maybe old Egon had fashioned the fireplace, or maybe some ancient mountain man had warmed himself there while the Civil War was fought or even the Revolutionary. His father taught him history in terms of the old stone fireplace and what was happening in the land while some man broke deadwood with his hands and piled it on dry needles on this very stone, Til, right here.

Til had made the plank floor and the roof piece by piece as he gathered lumber from town or used spare boards from the resort. He had made the chest that held his father's banjo and all the songbooks, the old yellow ones that had been here since he was a boy, and the new ones he had bought and memorized.

"Sew the pretty girls to my coattails, and down the road I'd go. Get along home . . ."

He went to the chest in automatic motion, reaching to

GERALD DI PEGO

64

touch the hand-carved lid as unconsciously as he would put his arm through a sleeve and step into a boot. It was part of his morning to touch the chest, but this morning, he opened it. He didn't often do that. He was wary of the chest, but the scents and sounds of this crystal morning had made him strong.

He knelt by the open lid and stared long and unafraid at the old yellow songbooks, the old banjo touched by his father, wood worn smooth by his father's fingers. He gently lifted the banjo from where it lay and cradled it against his chest. His fingers found the strings and frets but then became motionless. He held the instrument close against him. He closed his eyes.

He was a boy sitting cross-legged on the earthen floor of a lean-to. His father sat nearby, eyes closed, hands motionless on the old banjo.

"Cripple Creek, Dad."

"Wait. Shh."

"Remember it?"

"Shh."

His father was waiting for the song to play in his mind, hum through his body, reach his fingers. It came to him. The fingers moved. Til watched and smiled as the tinny notes scattered through the room like popping corn, joyful notes, tripping over each other in a rush, dancing notes the boy could almost see—and they came not from the strings. He watched closely and he knew—the notes came from his father's hands, like cards and coins from a magician. They sprang from his father's body and filled the room, filled the boy.

Til, now thirty-one and remembering, plucked the old banjo, plucked it again, keeping his eyes closed, moving his fingers more quickly now, thumbing a string, hammering another. Soon they were there in the cabin with him, that great bucketful of happy notes from "Cripple Creek," the same old notes his father had scattered here a hundred times. They were like old spoons spilling from the banjo, clanking and clattering on the floor, tiny old friends that drew Til back,

FOREST THINGS

back through years, back through all of the best moments. The fire was lighting a smile on his father's face and glinting off the banjo fittings. The crickets were drowned out and a song filled the forest. He smelled his father's pipe, burning pine logs, old blankets and sweet joy.

Til fought to hold on to the feeling, playing harder, faster, closing his eyes more tightly, closing his mind to The Memory that would soon be coming, clawing, screaming to get in.

He made a soft sound in his throat. His fingers fumbled on the strings. The Memory had pounced and torn through his defenses so easily—claws through paper. It was inside of him now. He was ten. It was night. He was screaming.

"Dad! Da-ad!"

Screaming until he had no more voice, and then screaming with his mind.

"Dad! Please! Where are you?!"

Til stopped playing the banjo. The last notes jumped out and bounced on the floor, and the silence that followed them was the most silence there could be, and the alone he felt was the most alone there was. Tears filled his throat. His hands shook as they carefully replaced the banjo and closed the lid of the chest. He closed it very gently, and then struck it with all his might.

Did you really leave me? And if you did, then why—why did you love me so hard for ten years? Why did you pull me so close and hold me so tight for ten years? Why didn't you leave right away like my mother? Why did you stay only to run away? Did you run away? Did you really leave me? And if you did, then why?

Til's father scratched a match alive and brought it to his pipe, sucked the flame away as Til, age ten, waited for the words he saw in his father's eyes. The mouth moved around the pipe stem, and the words floated down through sweet smoke.

"Warm cities . . . The cold stays up in the mountains like a wolf and never comes down. People drive up there and play

GERALD DI PEGO

in the snow and then drive down to summertime again. That's the place."

Did you go, Daddy? Did you go there? How could you go there and not take me with you? How could you leave me running behind you? You heard my steps, didn't you? You heard my voice.

"That's the place," his father said again, and the man's eyes dimmed. His body, leaning against a tree, did not move. He became as still as quiet water, water that reflects objects so sharply that the water itself seems to disappear. The boy was frightened, watching his father leaving him. He quickly thought of a question and threw it like a stone into the quiet water.

"Was my mom short? 'Cause I want to be tall."

The man sighed and leaned his head against the tree, back with his son again. "She was short, but she was young and still growin'. She's likely very tall now. Fact, I think I saw a picture of her. Looked like her, anyway. They got her in New York, out in the harbor, holding up a torch so the ships can find the city. Big tall lady."

"Aw, Dad."

"We might be in New York right now if I didn't have the chain on me."

"Chet could watch the business for a while, couldn't he?"

"It ain't the business." The business of refinishing and selling used furniture, the large metal building, the great tangle of cast-off tables, stoves, chairs and desks had been left to Lex Sharkis by his parents, both of them dead before they reached fifty. "It's the ghosts." The man pushed away from the tree and began knocking ash from his pipe. "I won't leave you any chains," he said, then he walked away. "Come on. Let's run awhile."

All you had to do was put out a hand, Dad, and take mine. I would've run with you anywhere. Did you think it over? Did the two possibilities battle in your mind? Take the boy. Leave him behind. Take him. Leave him. Or maybe you never

FOREST THINGS

thought at all, never left at all. Maybe you were running along one minute and changed the next, and you couldn't let me know. All you could do was shake the trees and whistle and moan and finger through my hair and blow warm on my face.

He suddenly pushed himself up, standing now, shaking himself, shaking the memory out of his mind. He paced. He sang. He tore open the door and stepped outside and slammed it behind him.

His song changed to whistling, then an absent humming, then it was gone. He studied the forest he was about to run through, took his one hopping step and was off.

The forest did not tremble at the rush of Til Sharkis, and the forest things did not scatter. His boot soles would tread only on grass and needles, deadwood and open ground. Leaves barely felt the brush of his clothes, and trees hardly noticed his passage. He was as familiar as the wind.

He charged a giant fallen tree, a huge downed dragon, stiffened by death. He leaped and landed lightly on the mossy trunk, leaped off and was running when he hit the ground.

He was nearly down to the resort, almost in flight when he heard it—someone was running with him, yards away. He glanced, but saw no one. He only heard and felt the presence. He smiled at the image of his father racing beside him. The image smiled and waved and disappeared.

Lyn Chase inched out of her bed, keeping her eyes on her brother. Allan didn't stir. There was no sound from her parents' room. The morning chill touched her bare legs, reached through her thin T-shirt and made her flesh tingle and her nipples grow hard. She shivered, slipping a pair of cutoff jeans over her panties. They were cut short and slit almost to her hip. She didn't snap them and didn't step into her sandals, didn't pull out a drawer to get a sweatshirt. Instead, she grabbed the shoes by their straps and moved silently to the door, opened it and closed it softly behind her.

When she was twenty feet from the cabin, she zipped and snapped her jeans and put on her sandals. She hugged her icey upper arms and walked into the forest to watch it change.

It had been a nighttime forest only moments ago, a place of menacing shapes and shadows, secret sounds, a black unknown. She was there for the transformation, watching the curtains drawn, the shapes identified, the sounds made innocent. She followed the daylight, moving deeper and deeper among the trees.

Birds greeted Lyn and the light with the same song. A squirrel paused to acknowledge them and then ran on. The treetops bowed to their presence. Good morning. Welcome.

Lyn's eyes were searching everywhere, seeing everything: long, thin branches, stretching armlike, sleeved with delicate lichen, wild flowers and feathery ferns revealing gems of dew to Lyn and the new sun. Look. For you. Welcome.

The girl moved as softly as the daylight and the forest awoke and greeted her without fear. She sat on a fallen tree and let the sun lay warm hands on her shoulders and back and arms, erasing the chill. Her body loosened and stretched. Her face relaxed. Her joy, carefully wrapped, protected, hidden, came forward. It was tentative, hesitant, wary at first, but it grew bold. It came to the front of her eyes and shined there, moist as the dewy forest. It eased her lips into a smile. She breathed in deeply and leaned back on the log, stretched her legs in front of her.

The forest was speaking to her quietly, with buzzing and birdsongs, tiny footsteps, the rattle of a woodpecker. A hundred eyes watched her. A warbler landed and marched bravely past her log. A chipmunk paused on hind legs to study her.

FOREST THINGS

Lyn's face, usually set and still, showed now that it could move and stretch in amazing angles. It could play. She copied the haughty look of the warbler and created expressions for the chipmunk that the animal had never seen. Her face was clay, pinched and punched by the invisible hands of an artist who could laugh.

Her mouth ran diagonally across her face, then opened wide as she pantomimed laughter that loosened her head and set it wobbling. She crossed her eyes, puffed her cheeks. The chipmunk twitched as though shaking his head in disbelief. Lyn's laughter was real now, part liquid, part whisper, but she was laughing. She stopped when she heard something strange. It was silence. The forest had quieted to listen. She listened too, and she rose. She saw the man.

Til Sharkis was at the horizon, running toward her, nearly flying through the forest, hardly making a sound. She hurried to the widest tree and hid behind it, watching him, her breath caught and her heart pounding.

His eyes studied the ground as he ran and his face was not tight with exertion, but peaceful and joyous. As he came close to her, she was filled with a wild urge to move.

She ran. She ran beside him separated by thirty yards, by trees and brush. She ran as fast as she could, her long legs pumping and her sandals slapping the ground, and she smiled and grew lighter.

She felt the steepness pulling at her and gave herself to it, watching for places to put her feet and hardly feeling them touch. It was a headlong, plunging run, and when fallen trees blocked her path, she leaped over them, and when a tangle of roots tilted the ground beneath her, she reached out to touch a tree for balance, but she missed.

She fell, tumbling over wet earth and brush and flowers and rotten wood, and she cried out.

Til heard her cry, and he knew. He changed the direction of his run, fighting the downhill pull, following the sound of her outcry. He came pounding to her, slowing and stopping, his chest heaving, his eyes searching her where she lay.

GERALD DI PEGO

70

She was on her back, propped on her elbows now, staring at him in pain and embarrassment. Her long legs were thrust at him from her slit jeans, and they showed slight scratches and deeper scrapes on both knees. She was stuck all over with wet needles and leaves. Her long hair lay on the earth like scattered red-brown ribbons, and her face was smeared with dirt.

To Til she seemed for a moment to belong there, something he had come upon in a walk through the woods, another forest thing, wet and rumpled and new, emerging with the morning.

She sat up as he knelt beside her. The Lyn who had been open and joyous now darted back inside and looked at Til from a distance, studied him with her deep and serious look, her eyes big and intense and a little afraid. She began straightening her clothes and then felt the pain in her elbow. She sucked in air and held it, her head dipping down, hiding her face.

"Let me see." He took her hand away from the hurt elbow and fingered gently about the bone. Air hissed through her teeth. "Can you move it?" She did. "Just a bruise, I guess," he said. Her face was still hidden, covered by her long hair. He picked out leaves that were tangled there—red-brown leaves from her red-brown hair.

He began to brush away the pine needles that stuck to her bare legs. His hand was light, barely touching her. When the hand moved up from her knees to the smooth flesh of her thighs, she drew her legs under to stand.

"Sit awhile. Let your body tell you if it hurts anyplace."

"I'm all right." But she did sit, and in a moment she stared at him through her embarrassment, past her shyness. "I was running with you."

"I know. Thought it was my father for a minute."

"Your father? He lives here?"

"Don't run in sandals. You have sneakers? Sneakers or boots."

She nodded, accepting the information in her serious way, storing it. "All right."

FOREST THINGS
———

"Lucky you didn't break a bone."

Her eyes were still on him, wondering. "Your father lives here?"

He got comfortable beside her, leaning back on wide-spread hands. "They say he left me—when I was ten. Here in the forest."

She waited, watching him, needing more. "They say?"

"Look."

He had leaned his head back, and she followed his eyes straight up, where the treetops were being ruffled by a wind she could not feel.

"I say he ran so fast he turned into the wind, and he never left me at all." He lay on his back, hands behind his head, staring upward.

Lyn watched him for a smile or a wink, but Til had spoken as if it were true. She too lay back on the wet earth and stared above. Her eyes changed color as she watched the wind—gray for the passing cloud, blue for the sky revealed, green for the top of the tree. Her eyes studied them all and found a place for them, kept them. When she turned to Til she saw that he had closed his eyes, and so she was able to study *him* too, tracing the outline of his face, watching his chest still heaving from the running, the heartbeat showing through his shirt. When he stirred, she looked away. In a moment she closed her eyes so that if he wanted to, he could study *her*.

He did move his gaze over her, slowly, blessing her small strong chin, her scraped knees, her long toes. "Got a pair of running shoes?"

She opened her eyes. "Yes."

He nodded and rose to his feet. He reached down and selected one of her long toes, gave it a good-bye tug. "See you later." He trotted away.

She lay for a while and watched the phantom wind.

GERALD DI PEGO

72

Til found them all gathered around the broken porch rail of cabin B—the Dermitters, the Widow, the Chases. They all turned to Til as he ambled out of the forest. Mrs. Chase came to meet him, worried.

"Have you seen Lyn? She was gone when we got up. Allan went down to the lake to see . . ."

"She's up the trail about half a mile."

"Doing what?" Chase's eyes were hard on Til.

"Taking a walk. Why?"

"The bear," Widow Rendon said. "He did this."

Til walked to the rail. Mag stood on the other side of it, moving close to the break as Til studied it. She was wearing a robe. The breeze from the lake gently opened her robe up to her thighs. She closed it. The breeze lifted the fabric again. She patted it closed, inches away from Til. His eyes jumped from the splintered railing to the woman's legs, from sharp spikes of wood to incredibly smooth flesh that asked for his fingers. He shook the loosened railing, glancing again at the robe, waiting for one more breeze. She was speaking to him, a smile in her words.

"I thought maybe he went up the mountains last night and ate you up."

"He's just a scrounger," Til said.

"Just a scrounger," Chase echoed him. "Well he's going to catch a bullet if he knocks on *my* door." He turned to Dermitter. "I've got a rifle you can borrow if you want."

"Yes! Christ! A cannon!" Dermitter laughed and his wife chuckled along but the others were too concerned—the

FOREST THINGS

Widow worrying about the cost of repairs, the Chases anxious about Lyn and Til growing angry at the game of the wind and the robe, the teasing breeze, Mag's hand now on the fabric, now off. Dermitter went on. "My God, first we get here and our car is thrown down a mountain. Now a bear is trying to move in with us."

"Mrs. Rendon'll have to charge you more for three in a cabin," Til said. The Dermitters liked that and laughed. Mag threw her head back and clapped once as if summoning the breeze. It came and exposed her legs up to the silky triangle of underwear. Til relaxed, satisfied.

"I'm worried about Lyn!" Mrs. Chase took slow half steps toward the forest, staring at the trail.

"The bear's just nosy," Til said. "He's not dangerous if you leave 'im alone."

"I'll go find her." Chase started off to his cabin.

"How you going to fix it, Sharkis? You took all my extra lumber for that cabin of yours."

"I took the *used* lumber."

"So do I have to buy new in town?"

"Some under the house." Til walked toward the lodge. The Widow followed. They stopped to watch Chase jog out the door of his cabin, carrying his bow and two hunting arrows.

"There's no season for bears," Til called after him. "They're protected." He walked on to the lodge.

Mag watched Til and the Widow walking away. "I wonder how long they've been here?"

"Prehistory," Michael said, and laughed. Mrs. Chase chuckled with her eyes still on the forest, waiting for Lyn.

Til dragged two boards out from under the lodge, feeling the Widow standing behind him. "This one'll fit."

"I'm making a stew," she said.

"Sounds good."

"You staying the night?" There was no weakness in her voice, a question but no sign of a plea. "That bed's not made up. If you're staying, I'll make it up."

He walked off to measure the railing. "I'm staying."

The resort was still by nine and dark by ten. It was nearly eleven when the sounds began, moans and cries still trapped, encased in flesh and bone, not yet finding a throat, lips, an inner voice humming in fear and ecstasy, a moving voice traveling from the room of the Widow Rendon down the hallway and into the room of Til Sharkis. There the voice found its way out and wailed fully into the still night.

It wasn't a sound to wake the sleeping, but Mag Dermitter was lying awake and listening, and she knew. This was passion. This was a woman with a man. This was the Widow— strong, tall woman—wrapped tightly against Til Sharkis— strong, graceful man.

FOREST THINGS

Mag felt tears in her throat. She wondered why. Loneliness? Yes, she wanted him, wanted him now, touching every part of her at once as she touched and tasted him. She wanted passion without words, without thought, without past or future.

She felt a tear slide down her face, and this one was made of jealousy. He was with the Widow. The Widow had no fire for him. She was cold. "I have the fire. Me. Mag." She whispered her name, and there were tears in her voice. These were made of fear. She had not escaped from that park outside her window. This was the same. There was life going on now in the dark lodge, and she was separated from it by panes of glass.

She turned on her side so that the tears would not choke her, tears of anger now, anger at allowing herself to be tamed, harnessed, held back for so many years—first by her parents, who cast looks at her like ropes, looks of shock, looks of disappointment, disapproval, great circles of rope that sailed over her head and fell over her shoulders, tightened around her. No, Mag. Don't Mag. Don't you dare. Later it was her husband casting the ropes as his eyes signaled to her. You're going too far, Mag. You're acting like a fool, Mag. Calm down, Mag. Take it easy. Easy.

The ropes had snapped two weeks ago as she and her husband had knelt together in the bed and watched the park. She was loose now. She would gallop.

She placed her hands on her face and swallowed tears made of hate. She hated her past and all those who had peopled it, including herself. She was loose now. She would gallop.

GERALD DI PEGO
———
76

Lyn Chase was dreaming a good dream, a cool and pretty dream of clear water and a quick silver fish swimming just below the surface and rising now, thrusting upward and bursting out of the water, emerging as a man, a hairy man who shook himself like a beast, his wet hair showering the sky with drops that exploded in the sun and blinded her. She was about to call to him when she felt a hand touch her bare stomach and slide downward slowly, the fingers pressing into her flesh, the hand moving under the silkyness of her panties and finding the silkyness of her hair.

She awoke with her own hand between her legs and the voice of the Widow Rendon coming to her across the dark yard. The voice was soft. It was the emotion in the voice that had invaded her dream and awakened her.

She held her breath to listen. The voice rose as the woman seemed to move within the lodge, come closer to a window—for the voice was clear now. It was singing in a language without words, first a wild song of ecstasy, then a soft song of peace.

Lyn slipped out of bed and went to stare at the dark lodge, at the window on the side of the building. Beyond there they held each other—Til and the Widow. He was inside of her. Lyn felt fear and wonder and the presence of something eternal. He was inside of her.

She waited for more sounds but there were none, then the floorboards creaked and she turned to see her father standing behind her in the dark.

FOREST THINGS

Chase whispered, "What're you doing?"

"Nothing."

They each stared into the shadowy form they knew to be the other's face. He must know, Lyn thought. He must have heard. "What was that, Dad?"

"Don't worry. Nothing."

"Somebody's voice."

"Somebody dreaming. You scared?"

"No." She turned again to the window, and he came beside her, looked out with her.

"Don't let that bear spook you."

"He won't, Dad."

"I'd hate to think he'd ruin our last week and a half."

"He won't."

The crickets gave a rhythm to the long silence.

"You like it here, Lyn?"

"Yes."

"You don't seem to."

She turned to him. They were still whispering. "Why?"

"You still don't do things with the family. I thought that this place . . . bringing everybody here would really make a family out of us. Doing things together, you know? But there's Lyn, still standing outside, being alone, going into the forest alone."

Her eyes drifted off to study the problem, examine all sides, find an answer in her serious way. "Dad, I'm not going away from anybody when I take my walks. I'm just . . . It's the thing I love most about being here."

"Why alone?"

"It . . . It's best alone."

"That's how it always is with you, and it's selfish. You should be with us, or when Allan and I go off, you should stay with Mom. She doesn't care for it here—she wouldn't say so, but . . ."

"She never wants to do anything."

"So, just stay with her."

Crickets. Crickets. Crickets.

GERALD DI PEGO

78

"Dad, lots of people like to take walks alone."

"I don't want you out there alone. Characters out there."

She could see his face clearly in the moonlight. He didn't turn to her. "Characters?"

He thrust his face toward the lodge. "Him."

She followed his look across the yard to the open window on the side of the building, the place where they both knew Til Sharkis lay with the Widow Rendon. "Him."

"He looks at you, you know."

She became aware then that she was wearing only panties and a loose tank top, became aware of so much of her own naked flesh, pure white in the window light. She leaned back into shadow.

"Of course you know."

"Dad . . ."

"Guys look and girls know."

Crickets. A night bird. The hiss of a breeze on the lake.

"I want you to do things with the family instead of standing outside, giving those looks of yours." He drowned out her protest. "I've got nine days before I have to go back to that goddamn job. I want those nine days to last a month, you know what I mean? I want peace. I want to store it up. I need it. What I don't need are problems when I go back. I don't want any problems here. From you. All right?"

"I just . . ."

"All right?"

His voice had risen to a dangerous pitch. She knew it well. Her ear had been tuned to it for sixteen years. She knew that in the next moment, if Lou Chase didn't get his way, he would move. His strong right hand would move against his problem and try to erase it. She had seen him wreck jammed machines, destroy telephones, smash furniture and toys, and she herself had been shaken, slapped and gripped hard by that hand. She had seen it push her mother across a room and knock Allan to the floor.

Her earliest memory was a picture of her father crouched over Allan's crib in the dark bedroom, lifting the crib off the

FOREST THINGS
———
79

floor and banging it down on its legs again and again—as the baby shrieked, as Mrs. Chase tried to pull her husband away and turn him toward herself so that she could absorb the anger and take the blows—and she did.

Lyn studied her father now in the moonlight. His hard eyes and hard mouth waited for an answer. Allan's answer would have been "Sure, Dad." Mrs. Chase would have said, "Of course, Lou, relax," and she would have forced a smile, hoping to coax a smile from him, to change his mood. Only Lyn could meet those hard eyes. She met them with the strong and serious look of a woman wrapped in a child's body, a child's pretty and fragile face. It was a deep look with pain in it and a strange kind of knowing.

Chase feared that look. It was the same look he had seen on her face when she was three years old and she had stared at him, watched him while he stood over the battered body of his wife in that dark bedroom. His wife lay moaning on the floor. Behind him his infant son was screaming. Standing before him was his tiny daughter, silent and staring, damning him.

Lyn said, "I'll ask Mom before I go walking, and . . ."

"Just stay with her."

"I won't go far so she can call me, Dad."

The man's hand was fast and sure. It found the soft flesh of her upper arm before she could pull back. It gripped hard. He whispered. "You never give me any peace." He knew he was hurting her. It showed in her eyes, but those eyes didn't leave him. He pulled her toward him, slowly, until their faces were inches apart. "Bitch."

Her face softened, blurred, ready for crying. The tears came silently as he released her and she leaned back out of the light.

He stared at her awhile, then turned and walked carefully through the darkness to his bedroom, went inside.

Lyn came forward to the window and looked at the lodge again. Her hand moved absently on her face, rubbing the tears into her skin.

GERALD DI PEGO
————
80

Allan whispered from his bed. "Why do you always make him mad?"

She didn't answer. She wondered if Allan had heard the wild nightsong from across the yard. "What woke you up?"

"You and Dad. You always get him into a lousy mood."

"He always is."

"You make it worse. He probably won't take me fishing tomorrow. He'll get up early and go alone."

"I'm sorry."

"Sure."

She turned to the darkness that spoke with Allan's voice. "Anyway he fishes *for* you. He takes the rod out of your hand . . ."

"I'm learning," the darkness said.

"He won't let you." She heard him stir and then go silent. She could read her brother's thoughts and feel his sorrow. She could see the pictures his mind was making, images of his father, impatient, disapproving, grabbing the fishing rod from his hand, the shovel, the bow, the gun, the pencil, the bat— "Here, Christ, I'll do it. Watch." And Allan *would* watch and try again, feeling ashamed, aching for approval. Lyn ached for Allan and felt her tears coming again. "If he doesn't take you," she said, "come with me. We'll walk up the mountain."

Still the darkness didn't move, didn't speak. Then it whispered, "I wish you had stayed home."

Mag was up and dressed, staring at her sleeping husband, studying him as if he were an acquaintance from long ago. His hair was lighter than it had been. When had it changed? His face, sagging with sleep, was heavier than she remembered. She studied him as morning shined

FOREST THINGS
───────

full into the cabin. He didn't stir. He didn't know. He was only part of her past now. He was of long ago.

She hoped he would stay asleep. She needed time without him. She wished he would sleep for two weeks and let her have the vacation, the forest and the lake and the mountains —without him.

She heard the screen door of the lodge bang shut, and she went to her window. It was Til. He paused to study the sky a moment, then he took a hopping step and began to jog toward the mountain trail.

Mag opened the door and stepped out on the porch. She saw him trotting on, disappearing into the forest. She stepped down from the porch and ambled toward the lake, making a half circle, turning slowly toward the forest and the trail, looking about and moving casually as though she weren't following him.

The steepness of the trail pulled at Mag's legs and tried to hold her back. Branches barred her way and roots hoped to trip her. Her husband said, "What do you think you're doing?!" with his eyes. Her parents cast disapproving looks that never reached her. Her anger was a sail. She blew up that mountain trail like a storm, arms reaching out ahead of her, teeth bared. "I am walking through the forest. I am following a man. I am loose now. I shall gallop."

"Hi."

His voice panicked her for an instant, and the face she turned to him was tight with alarm and with the anger that was helping her up the mountain. Her teeth were still bared, and there was a fury in her eyes that soon softened and dissolved in surprise and embarrassment. Til was sitting beside the trail. She had passed him without seeing him. "God, you really spooked me. I didn't see you . . ."

He patted the log beside him. She sat lightly, two feet from him.

GERALD DI PEGO

"I thought I'd try the trail. Such a great morning. You're up early." Slow down, she told herself. He probably knows you followed him. He probably knows you listened to him last night. Look at him looking at you. He knows.

But Til's eyes weren't ridiculing. They were pleased with her, and his body moved on the log to welcome hers.

"Hear him last night?"

Her face flushed. "Who?"

"The bear."

"Oh." She smiled and shook her head. "No, I heard something. Sounds . . ." She trailed off and then decided, no, go on. Say it. Do not hold back. Not anymore. "I heard sounds from the lodge last night. Mrs. Rendon. Did you hear it?"

He looked off into the forest. "She dreams sometimes."

"I heard her moving around."

He looked at her. "She walks sometimes, while she's dreaming."

"Where does she go?"

She wasn't stopping. Til began to smile, studying her. You wouldn't keep your eyes closed, would you, he thought. You'd look at me. You'd burn me with those eyes. We'd go up in smoke. She answered his smile, looked away. He took the opportunity to run his eyes along her profile, down her body. She hadn't replaced the button on her denim shirt. Today her bra was white and just as lacy. He thought of the flesh it held. He thought of her thighs beneath the tight cloth of her jeans. Her body seemed to be willing itself out of its clothes. It wanted freedom, and he felt it wanted his touch. She had heard him last night with the Widow. She wanted him. He was sure, and his body was just as willing, as eager. "Where are *you* going?" he said.

"Just for a walk."

"So fast? Thought you were chasing somebody."

"No. Now, your turn. Where are *you* going?" She turned those eyes on him, eyes dancing with humor and something else, something desperate.

FOREST THINGS
_____

83

He smiled and stood up. "Swimming. Water's ice cold but clean."

"The lake is the other way."

"Mountain water. A stream. Just a trickle this time of year, but the beavers dammed it and made me a swimming pool." Oh, how we would hiss if we hit that cold water. Our naked bodies would raise steam and in that steam we'd come together. Jesus. He thought of asking her to come with him, a married woman he hardly knew, her husband just a mile away, to come with him and strip and swim.

She felt his eyes asking her to come and her chest tightened, her heart beating faster. What if he did ask her? What should she do? Maybe he was cruel. Maybe he would talk to his friends about the easy woman from the city.

The fun of asking her, the joy of all the possibilities fought with common sense in Til's mind. Joy spoke and said, "Come with me."

Panic answered, "Oh, no thanks, I . . . should be getting back."

He nodded, shrugged. "Another day."

Her smile was stiff as she rose and nodded, waved to him and started back down the trail.

"See you later."

"Yes," she said. She was ten steps away and already hating herself, ashamed of herself. This was a moment. You let it escape. Where was the strength? Where was the will? Should I turn now and say, "Wait a minute. I'll swim with you"? No. It's too late. You're too far. The mountain is pulling you down, making you run away. If you look back now you'll double your shame, silly woman, weak woman. This was a moment.

GERALD DI PEGO

She was marching stiff-legged, fighting the steepness of the trail, when she met the children, Lyn and Allan, coming toward her. The hate that she carried inside, attacking herself, sprang at them, at those young faces, new eyes. She wanted to stop them, to stretch wide across the trail and bar their way, threaten them with teeth and claws, make them run back to their holes. Do not go up the trail. Do not meet with him. Leave him alone. I failed today, but I won't tomorrow. Go back. She tried to soften her face. She hoped she was smiling as she reached them.

"Hi. Beautiful morning."

"Yes," Lyn said. Allan smiled shyly. They moved off the trail to let her pass.

Lyn turned to watch Mag taking stiff, hard steps down the steep trail, her dark hair bouncing. "You see how she looked at us?"

"I think we scared her," Allan said. "Maybe she saw the gun." He was wearing the .22 revolver holstered at his side. He unsnapped the guard and drew the weapon as they walked on.

"She wasn't scared. She was mad—at us, at me!"

FOREST THINGS

"She doesn't even know you."

"What're you doing? You're not going to shoot, are you?"

"It'll keep the bear away, Dad said."

"It'll keep everything away. Don't you want to see a deer or something?"

Allan was taking aim at the trunk of a pine. Then he holstered the gun, paused and drew it quickly.

"Jesse James."

"I could hit that bear from the hip. Hit 'em in the head." He cocked the hammer and drew a bead on a fat pine cone halfway up the tree. "See that big cone?"

Lyn followed the gun barrel. "Please don't shoot, Allan."

"I bet I can knock it down."

"Come on, Let's keep walking."

"Dad said I can practice."

"I don't want to hear it."

It was as though the black hole of the gun barrel was throwing a narrow beam of light up into the tree, an invisible light, but a beam that the tree could feel, a moving beam that traced a slow pattern in the branches, found the cone, settled on it. The cone trembled in the invisible light. The branch shuddered. The entire tree tensed for the shock.

Lyn stared at the dark cone and the branch and the invisible connection between them.

The tree drew itself in, a microscopic shrinking.

Lyn sucked in air, a gasp of wonder. The pine cone had detached and was falling. Allan had not fired. The great seed hit the forest floor and bounced and rolled and settled.

Allan turned to her, amazed and suspicious. "Lyn!"

"It just fell."

They walked to the cone and stared at it. Allan's eyes came back to his sister. There was some fear in his look, and the fear made him angry. "Jesus, Lyn."

"They're always falling."

He holstered the gun and walked on. She watched him go. Then she knelt down and touched the rough cone. She gently rolled it under her hand, nestling it deeper into the carpet of

GERALD DI PEGO

86

needles and loose earth. In a moment she left it and followed her brother.

When she caught up, he was standing still, looking off into the forest and waving for her to stop. He whispered. "Listen. Listen."

"What?"

"Shh. Listen."

"Where?"

"Damnit, Lyn, shut up."

She turned her head an inch at a time, straining to hear. In a moment there was a definite rustle of leaves far to their right. They looked at each other.

"The bear, I bet," Allan said.

"Could be deer."

"Could be Bigfoot."

They listened again. There was movement, something large. Lyn started toward it.

"Lyn, we shouldn't go too far off the trail."

"We won't. I just want to see it." She looked back. Her brother hadn't moved. "Allan? We'll just look from far away."

They moved slowly, carefully, following the sounds, ad-monishing each other with sharp looks when one of them tripped or snapped a twig. They stopped, listening, turning toward each other with unfocused eyes, waiting. Then they heard it again, farther on, and they smiled in common ex-citement, moving forward. Something was hurrying ahead of them, just out of sight.

Lyn was wearing sneakers, and they carried her silently around the trees and over fallen logs. She had to hold herself back. Her feet, her heart, wanted to run through the forest as Til had run, but she didn't want to frighten the creature ahead of her. She walked quickly, her brother beside her. She was filled with the certainty that the next three steps would bring her close enough to see what they were following, then the next five steps, then certainly when they reached that rise in the land.

FOREST THINGS

They stopped on the rise and lay on their stomachs. They could see a pond of clear water and hear the gurgle of a small stream. Something moved beyond the trees, approaching the water. They held their breaths.

Til Sharkis emerged from the trees, naked, walking to the pond.

Lyn and Allan stared a moment, then the boy turned away, embarrassed. He began to move back down the rise of land, the way they had come. He looked at his sister, but she hadn't moved. He whispered, "Lyn!" but she shook her head, no, as she stared at the man. Allan turned to the pond again.

Til was in the water up to his knees, stiff and blowing with the chill of it. He cupped water in his hands and splashed it on his legs and shoulders.

Lyn studied his body, his hairy chest and back, the curve of his buttocks (so white next to the deep tan of his back), his strong thighs, and the front of him now as he turned toward her, the curly hair and loose flesh between his legs, his penis angling to the side a bit and bobbing as he moved. She pressed low to the ground, staring. She felt her brother beside her. Til moved into the water just over his waist, then he submerged for an instant and came bursting out, shaking himself like an animal, his hair and beard scattering drops that exploded in the sun.

Here was the man-fish-beast from last night. Lyn realized she had been dreaming forward again, and she felt a mix of awe and dread at her power to see ahead.

It had been Til alive inside her dream, moving exactly as he moved now, and it had been Til inside her own hand when she had touched between her legs. He had touched her there last night with her own fingers, raising the same sense of mystery and desire she felt now.

Til stood in the waist-high water, his back to them, his hands moving lazily, paddling. "Come on in, you two," he said.

They rose, their mouths open, faces flushing red. When he

GERALD DI PEGO
———
88

turned to them, they slid down the rise and ran, leaving behind them the laughter of the creature who had led them through the forest.

Mag stood still with her hands hanging in front of her, one trapping the other by the wrist. Even her eyes barely moved, afraid to break something. She was in the Widow's kitchen without invitation.

"Comfortable in there; beds okay?"

"Oh, yes, I . . ."

"Those are almost new mattresses. You try the oven yet?"

"Everything's fine, Mrs. Rendon. I just . . . You know, I thought we'd get acquainted. This is such a lovely old place."

" 'Bout fifty years old. Took a lot of fixing up when my husband and I bought it. Everything's in good shape now. If you need extra blankets, I've got some."

"No, we're very comfortable."

"Why don't you come in the living room."

The Widow led Mag down the hall. They passed a dark bedroom on their right. "That's my room there." And a small sunny one on the left. "Til stays there."

Mag halted and took it in, breathed it in—his room. It was a small room, filled by the bed and an old armoire, a dresser, frayed rug on the floor, old bentwood rocker standing motionless, balanced, waiting.

She quickly placed him there, sat him in the chair and set it rocking, the wood crackling as it became comfortable with his body. She made the bed creak with his weight, watched him lying on the quilt, first clothed, then naked.

FOREST THINGS
───────
89

The Widow was watching her. She walked on into the living room.

They sat on musty furniture in a room that smelled of wood and smoke. "Just you and Til run this whole place?"

"Not much to run." The Widow's eyes were blue marble, smooth and cool. She had seen Mag in Til's doorway, and she knew. "I can make us some coffee."

"No, I'll just stay a minute."

"You and your husband from New York City, are you?"

"Yes. This is so much nicer. Peaceful. Clean."

"My husband and I always kept it clean."

"Was that a long time ago, I mean when he died?"

"Twelve years."

"Oh. Well, I admire you, handling things yourself. Of course, Til is a big help, I imagine."

"Good handyman."

"Have you known him long?" Mag was charging straight ahead. To hell with marble-eyes. The woman didn't own him. How could she own him, keep him, please him with hard eyes like that, with white hair, with fifty years of time scratched into her face and dragging on her body. I'm twenty-nine. My body is ready now. My spirit is ready. I have left old people, old places, old selves behind me. I will be new for him.

The Widow paused a moment. "Since he was a boy. He'd come up the mountain with his father."

"Funny, isn't it, to watch a person grow like that—boy to man. At first I thought he might be your son or nephew or . . ."

"No relation."

Go ahead, stare, with your lips tight and small and your eyes freezing me. I won't let you keep him. You've had him. You're old. I want him. He wants me. Have you seen him look at me? You can have him again when I leave, but he may not want you—after me. "So then he's lived all his life on this mountain. What a life—so . . ."

"No. He's lived other places. Been in the army. He likes it here."

"I'm sure he does. And you?"

GERALD DI PEGO

"It's where I'm going to be buried." Chilly blue marble. The Widow sat with a straight back, straight face that didn't move.

Mag looked about and smiled. "Well . . . I envy you. You've really got something here." She was left to fill the silence with her empty smile. She rose. "I guess I'll get back now." She turned to the hallway.

The Widow gestured to the front door. "You can go out this way." She began walking to the door.

Mag wanted to hurry down the hallway and pause for one more look—his rug, his chair, his pillow. But the Widow was opening the front door. She brushed by the woman, smiling. "See you again soon."

"Anything you need in the cabin, just come and tell me." The Widow stepped out on the porch and watched Mag leave, watched her glance at the window on the side of the lodge— Til's window.

The Widow Rendon turned to the lake even before she was conscious of the sound. He was there in the boat coming across the water. Maybe he would sleep at the lodge tonight. Maybe she would dream that dream of the beast tonight. She could dream it only when he was there, breathing in his bed, twelve steps down the hall. She felt the beast's strong arms and legs wrap around her. She closed her eyes. When she opened them, they had softened to silk.

"Try it again."

Allan reeled in his line, a bit shamefaced. His cast had gone only half as far as his father's. They were fishing from large rocks on the shore of the lake. Lyn had climbed to

FOREST THINGS
———

the highest rock and lay flat on the sun-warmed stone, her chin in her hands, watching her father and brother.

Allan cast again, paying close attention to his wrist, his thumb, his stance. His thin face was set, lips pursed in concentration. Still his bobber plopped into the water only fifteen feet from his rock. His father's line had hit a mark a good thirty-five feet out where the lake deepened.

"Leave it."

Allan sat down, watching his bobber for a bite, composing his long and somber face so as not to show the shame there.

Lyn stared hard at the back of her father's head, concentrating on three words, trying to push them into her father's brain so that he would think they were *his* words, so that he would speak them—Good cast, Allan.

He didn't speak them, and Lyn turned away to watch the water. The lake was as much of a mask as her brother's face. She wasn't fooled. There were fish under there, like a thousand dark thoughts swimming and waiting. Someday they would break the surface and become words. Minnows would be tiny words; long fish would be long words; fish with teeth would be angry words; and clams—they would be whispers. When the lake finally spoke its thoughts, she wondered, what would it say?

Her eyes lifted to the horizon. The wide gray lake was being torn like a page as Til brought the motorboat across the center, coming home with mail and supplies. Lyn watched, placing herself in the boat, feeling the wind in her face, smiling through the wind at Til who smiled back. Her mind sent words out across the lake to meet him. I have shoes. I have shoes for running.

"He's gonna scare the fish," Allan said.

"What fish?" Chase said it with more anger than humor, but Allan giggled. "The fish in these lakes are invented by public relations people, travel agents. Phony fish. I've never seen such a summer for lousy fishing. What're you doing? Don't move it unless you've got a bite."

GERALD DI PEGO
<hr>

"I was gonna cast again, Dad."

"Leave it. That is what scares the fish—all your practice casting. Might as well throw stones in the water. I doubt if we'll get one nibble."

"I think so," Lyn said from above. "I dreamed about cleaning fish. Somebody was cutting a head off."

Her father's look stopped her. His anger had jumped from the lake to his son, now to his daughter. "Oh, wonderful," Chase said. "You dreamed us some fish."

Allan added his stare to his father's, admonishing her.

Chase went on. "That's great. Thank you. What kind?"

"Just a head of a . . ."

"A trout? What did it look like? Come on, be specific."

"It was a dream, Dad. I . . ."

"Well, your goddamn dreams take all the suspense out of life, Lyn. I mean, why should I fish if I *know* I'm going to catch fish because my daughter dreamed it for me?" Chase was reeling in his line. "Takes all the fun out of it. So the hell with it."

Allan slumped on his rock. "Aw, Da-ad."

Chase was gathering his gear. "I'm leaving. Then it can't be true, right, Lyn? Huh? Just by walking away I can make your dream nothing. Just a dream like everybody else's kind of dream, right?"

Chase was stepping and jumping across the rocks, heading for the sand, aiming for the lodge.

Allan cast Lyn a hard look that landed on the mark. "You know he hates you talking about your dreams."

She watched her father trace a swerving path over the rocks, looking down, moving as though he followed directions written on the ground—two steps this way; hop to that rock; jump to here. She tried to stare into his mind, to push words in there for him to say—See you at the cabin. See you for lunch, kids—but the words bent and broke on that strong face, that thick, straight black hair. He didn't turn or wave or speak. She kept trying until she heard her brother gasp.

FOREST THINGS

Allan had a fish. His line was taut, and his pole bent down toward the water like a trembling finger following the fish, pointing—here! Here! Here!

Allan shouted. "Dad!"

"Let Dad go." Lyn knelt above him.

"Dad! Wait!"

"Let him go, Allan! You can get the fish."

"He's big!"

"You can get him."

"Get the net!"

"You!"

Allan fought the fish closer and closer to his rock. Then he knelt down and let go of the pole with one hand to grasp the landing net. He nearly fell from the rock, and he cried out, but he got the net under the fish and stood up, bringing the thrashing, panicked bass with him. He held the net up toward his sister, the wet mesh dripping diamonds in the sunlight. "Look!" It flopped and jumped in wild frenzy, twenty inches of desperate fish-life. "Look!"

Lyn looked at Allan's face, at the awe and pleasure crowded into corners by the giant smile. She yelped and slid down to his rock and hugged him.

"Look at it!" He still held it up, unbelieving. Then he turned to her, suddenly afraid, wondering. "Did I catch it just because you dreamed it?"

"No. I dreamed it because you were going to catch it. All by yourself."

His grin flashed again. He placed the fish on the rock to string it. "Can't wait to show Dad!"

Lyn's smile faded and her eyes, bright with pleasure, went to gray.

GERALD DI PEGO
_____

94

Til sat on the porch steps of the lodge and let evening ease into night around him. All color faded with the light. All light faded but the moon. He could hear the Widow inside the lodge, moving about, cleaning away the leftover pieces of the day and throwing them away. Only when the garbage lid had banged down over the last bits of Tuesday, could Tuesday night officially begin. There. She was finished. The water faucet in the kitchen squeaked off. He heard her tread down the hall, into her room. She would undress and choose a gown for the night. She would lie down and wait for the dream to raise her. Everything was in its place. Tuesday was in the garbage. Til was in the lodge. She would close her eyes and wait.

Til leaned back and stretched his legs down the steps. He thought of the Widow lying long and straight in her bed, and he blessed her. He wished she were sitting beside him. He wished she would look at him, talk to him tonight when she came to him. He knew she wouldn't, but he blessed her anyway.

He glanced at the cabins and imagined Lyn Chase in her bed, her big eyes still open, still pondering and storing all that happened in the day. Turn. Go to sleep. He saw her turn on her side and draw up her knees, close her eyes. He blessed her, and he blessed Mag and wondered how she slept. Was she making love with her husband? Did they fall asleep holding each other or turn away, back to back? He blessed all the huddled forms in all the beds as far as he could see, across the

FOREST THINGS

lake and up the mountains. He drew the big starry quilt over them all, and then he rose and walked into the lodge and went to bed.

The wind came first that night, before sleep, before any sounds from the Widow's room. First there was the wind, blowing clouds across the moon, deepening the darkness, awakening the water in the lake, shaking the trees that wanted rest, teasing and tormenting, causing chaos. The lake water slapped at the dock. The trees moaned. The garbage can fell and lost its lid. Bits of Tuesday were released and whipped about the yard. Doors shook, and the window of Til's room rattled.

He stopped breathing to listen for another rattle of glass. It was as if the wind had grown a hand, knuckles, fingers. The rattle came again, and Til sat up in bed and looked and gasped.

There was a face there, someone staring through the window, with eyes wild and afraid, someone retreating slowly, back into darkness. It was Mag's face.

Til went to the window and opened it. Clouds hid the moon. The yard was a deep heavy black, and he saw only a shape, a wildly moving shape. He stared hard. The shadow became Mag. The movement was the flapping and billowing of her robe as the wind tried to take it from her. She stood still, clutching the robe, staring at him, frightened.

He stepped through the window and jumped lightly to the grass of the yard. He was naked, and the wind was warm on his body. He came close to her. She was nearly naked too, for the impatient wind was tearing at her. This was no tease, no game. He came close enough to see her eyes. There was more than fear there. There was a hunger that was as deep and driving as his own. There could be no words, for the wind would have snatched them and thrown them away. The gusts were eager, violent, pushing them closer.

Til took the single step that brought them together. He put his arms around her and felt her tense and then let go, come hard against him, hold him. They kissed with lips, tongues and teeth, and, as they kissed, the wind took hold of her robe and spread it so that Til felt her nakedness against his flesh.

He slid an arm down in back of her knees and lifted her, carried her easily around to the front of the lodge, between the building and the beach where there were trees and the deepest shadows.

He laid her on the grass and knelt over her and felt her arms slide around his neck. She pulled him close. They grappled and turned—hungry mouths, hungry hands. With his fingers and thighs and lips he felt every inch of the body he had only glimpsed before, the body he had wanted. It belonged to him now as his body belonged to her.

He grabbed the flesh of her buttocks in a grip that should have made her scream, but she only moaned, her mouth against his chest, her teeth finding muscle and biting hard and deep, bringing pain he hardly felt as they turned in the grass, as he gathered his fist into the hair between her legs, as she held his thickened organ and guided it inside of her.

When the frenzy had reached its peak, when their minds dissolved and their bodies threatened to break apart, the release came, and with it their outcries. Til roared and trembled. Mag moaned and began to cry and to laugh.

Sobbing and laughing she held him as they rolled again on the soft earth, and again. I made this happen, her mind screamed. I made this happen. I wanted him and made him want me, and I gave to him and made him give to me, and it was without words or thoughts, past or future. It was what I wanted, and I made it happen. I am loose. I am galloping.

Til had never felt a passion as furious as Mag's. No one had

FOREST THINGS
———
97

ever cleaved to him so strongly and attacked so hungrily. It was a passion equal to his own. It was total—and it could be, it might be, what he had ached for and searched for. Tonight, he thought, he might have found the opposite of alone.

The Widow felt the pulse of the night speed crazily, driven by the mad wind. The dream of the beast came leaping at her, rushing as fast as the night, gripping her, pulling her.

She lunged out of bed and across the room, eyes closed, groping for her door and opening it. She cried out, stumbling into the hall, hurried and harried by great gusts that shook the lodge and screamed through holes and cracks in the walls. She half ran, her breathing audible now, moans and cries coming always faster.

She felt her way into Til's room and lurched toward the bed.

No hands caught her. Her knees struck the mattress, and she fell forward, her hands flung out to protect her, her large, wide-spread hands clutching pillow and quilt. She halted a moment—with the night rushing wild through her soul. She let her hands roam the bed. It was empty.

Her breath was released in a sob. She waited, but the beast did not touch her, take her. Perhaps he was watching her, tormenting her, punishing her. She should look. She should find him. He's behind her. He's in the corner. She listened for breathing but heard none.

If she looked, if she opened her eyes, she admitted everything. She lost the protection of blindness, the innocence of sleep, she destroyed the myth of the dream. Is that what he

GERALD DI PEGO

98

wanted? Was he waiting and watching for that? Was that his price?

She waited, but still no strong fingers, no smell of him. She shuddered and sobbed again. She opened her eyes.

The room was empty. She covered her face and fled, knowing the way best by darkness.

Til had withdrawn from Mag, and she had rolled over on her stomach. The robe was bunched around her shoulders. He pulled it down and covered her, wrapped her in it as he turned her over. He stared at her face, and through the dark he thought he saw her smile.

She sat up and tried to stand. Her legs gave way. He rose and helped her. They steadied and swayed there in the dark wind, staring at shadows. He moved close to hold her again, but she slipped away, backed away from him and then hurried across the yard toward her cabin.

Mag entered her cabin and softly closed the door. She stood still a moment, remembering how she had felt when she was about to leave, about to cross the yard to Til's window. She had been terrified, but she had

FOREST THINGS

willed herself to go, and the night had helped her, the wind had pushed her. Now it was done. She was back, and she was new, a different Mag, and Michael didn't even know she had been away.

She went close to her husband. He was heavy with sleep. She went to a chair and sat on the edge of it a moment to think, to plan. She should wash herself, hide her soiled robe. Were there marks on her body? She almost laughed aloud, covering her mouth, giddy with the memory of what she had done. She turned to her husband and whispered, "I walked across the yard." His heavy breathing did not change. "I knocked on his window. I really did, Michael." He was deep asleep. She went close to him. "I thought he would go to the door—but you know what he did? He came right out the window. He came outside naked, and we made love on the grass, wild love, Michael." He didn't stir. She laughed again and this time did not cover her mouth.

She went to the small kitchen area and turned on the light, put water on to boil, prepared a cup with instant coffee. The pan banged on the stove; the cup rapped on the counter top; the spoon rang against the cup. In a moment she heard Michael's voice, soft, broken, torn from sleep.

"Mag?"

She giggled silently, her stomach throbbing with laughter until it hurt.

"Mag? What . . .?"

She came close to the bed. "Can't sleep. Can you hear that wind? I just had to go out. It's wonderful out there. But I fell. Look. I'm a mess." She sat on the bed. "And my ass'll be bruised; I'm sure. I'm sorry I woke you."

"That's okay, I . . . Jesus. What time . . .?"

"It's not late, really. About midnight. Do you want coffee?"

He had risen up on one elbow. He now flopped back against the pillow, closed his eyes. "Coffee? Christ. I want sleep."

She hurried to the kitchen and turned off the stove, turned

GERALD DI PEGO

———

100

out the light. "Michael . . ." she came back to the bed and sat beside him. "Michael, since you're awake. Hey . . ." She kissed him softly. He opened his eyes halfway. "Michael." She kissed his slack lips again, pushing her tongue between them.

"Jesus, Mag."

She laughed, slipping out of her robe. She pulled the blanket off him, and then the sheet.

"I don't believe this."

She laughed again, lying on top of him, sliding her fingers into his hair, moving his head from side to side. "Come on. Wake up."

"Jesus, give me a . . ."

She covered his mouth with her own, silencing him. She rubbed her legs against him. He grabbed her buttocks and she smiled in pain. He moved his hands up and down her back, but slowly.

She sat up, straddling him and rocking now. "Michael . . ."

"Slow down."

"No! Come on. Michael. Michael."

He took her breasts and pulled, drew her down to him. She kissed him again and again, still rocking with her pelvis, and whispering now. "Yes, come on. Michael. Let's. I'll say, 'Oh my God,' I will. Michael."

Always before in their lovemaking, if she had been too quick, too strong, her desire too apparent, he would have difficulty. Now, with her new fury, he had no chance. She knew this. She did not stop. "I'll say it, Michael. I know I will. I'll scream it like I used to. 'Oh my God.' Please."

She felt him trying and then stop trying. He held her shoulders and pushed her back from his face. He looked wounded. His voice was soft.

"I can't right now. Give me some time."

She sat on him again. She smiled and stroked his chest.

"Christ, I just woke up."

"It's okay. Really." She moved off him and pulled up the sheet and blanket, covered him. "I'm sorry. You sleep now."

FOREST THINGS

101

But his wounded eyes would not close. "Just give me some time."

"Michael." She kissed him. "It's okay. Really." She lay down beside him on top of the covers, an arm across his chest.

"You woke me from a sound sleep."

"Shhhhh." She moved her hand over the blanket that covered his chest. She stroked his face lightly. In a moment he turned on his side, turned away from her and closed his eyes. She watched his body a long while, watched it slowly slacken and fall asleep. She smiled at his back and her smile was not kind to him. It was a good-bye smile.

The morning light at Til's window told him eight o'clock at least. He sat up in bed and rubbed his face, scratched his head and shook it. Eight o'clock and no kitchen sounds. Where was the Widow? She hadn't come to him last night, or she had come and found him gone. He would know by her eyes.

He dressed slowly, examining his bite wounds and scratches, touching some of them, remembering and wondering. Would Mag come to him again? He wouldn't wait to see. He would go to her.

He scuffed into the kitchen and was startled by the Widow. She sat at the table, dressed and combed, sat over a cup of coffee gone cold. She looked at him with nearly empty eyes, and he knew.

"Mornin'."

She nodded. Just the faintest powder blue was all her eyes could manage.

GERALD DI PEGO

Til felt guilty and then angry. She hadn't spoken to him yesterday evening. She hadn't whispered, "I'll come to you tonight." Never in three years had she said that. She would only come dream-walking and blind and expect to bump into him like a chair in the dark, like a wall. He went to the refrigerator.

"Sit down," she said. "I'll get to it in a minute."

He poured coffee for them and sat. She was silent.

"Thought I'd see if they'd all like to hike up the mountain, have lunch at the top. Maybe today, tomorrow."

She nodded. "Make sure nobody breaks his neck."

There was no sound and nothing moving but the steam from the coffee.

He sighed. "I'm sorry about last night."

His words were like a slap. Her eyes went wide, went bright blue with anger. She rose quickly and opened the refrigerator, began the motions of the morning, knowing hands reaching out independently, selecting, assembling—eggs, flour, milk, bacon—flowing from one job to the next in unconscious routine—cabinet door, bowl, drawer, beater, sugar.

"Edith . . ." He seldom used her first name. She didn't seem to hear. "Talk to me."

She went on, expressionless, a silent brain commanding hands, feet, a mind ticking down a list. Til wasn't on the list. He had no part in her morning. He was absent.

He stood up and went to the back door. "Not hungry," he said, going out.

He walked into the forest. Almost nine, the sky said. He spread his arms wide in a shrug and let them fall and slap his sides. He shook his head and muttered. He picked up a long, dead stick and swung it against a tree, shattered it, threw the stump of it far into the forest.

It hit and frightened something. He heard a light-footed skittering. "Sorry," he called out. "Sorry, there, John Deer, Jane Doe, fawn, rabbit, whoever the hell . . ."

He stopped because the skittering had led his eyes to a clearing, and in the clearing stood Lyn Chase.

FOREST THINGS

She raised a hand halfway, in a half wave, studying him with her careful, serious eyes.

"Hi." He jogged to her. "What're you up to?"

She was holding a long blue towel. She held it up, a bit embarrassed. "Swimming . . . where *you* were."

"Oh, yeah. Can you find the place?"

"I think so."

"I'll take you there."

He started out and she followed, then caught up to him. "My father thinks I'm down at the lake so . . . I have to go fast."

He looked at her as they walked, and he smiled, walking faster, then hopping once and breaking into his run.

She ran with him, sometimes in perfect step, the two of them leaping a fallen tree, landing, running on in rhythm. He glanced at her, saw her long hair trailing, saw joy sparking somewhere in those big deep eyes, saw the faintest smile.

They thudded up to the pond, out of breath, sending birds into the air, driving woodchucks, mice and beavers to cover.

She walked to the water's edge and began unbuttoning her shirt. He wondered if she expected him to look or to turn away and leave now. He noticed her neck was flushed red.

She took off the shirt, and Til smiled and sat down on the bank. She was wearing a bathing suit, a red bikini. She was careful sliding her cutoff jeans down over her buttocks, keeping the suit in place. She stepped into the water and her small face, her pretty, set, still face went wild, mouth and eyes popping wide.

Til laughed aloud. "By about two o'clock the sun warms it up nice." He laughed again, watching her tight, hunching walk into the water. She smiled too, turning away from him, gasping as the icy water touched her stomach. She hopped for a while on the muddy bottom, then suddenly squatted down, the water rising to her chin.

"There you go." He watched her a moment, then leaned back and looked up at the sky and the distant mountains. He

GERALD DI PEGO
___

104

felt like a quick plunge into the water, but he thought his nakedness would frighten or embarrass her, and he didn't want that. He liked the feeling of her in the pond, enjoying herself, enjoying the forest. He felt as if she were his guest here, and he was happy to share this place with her. He knew she appreciated it. "Like the forest, do you?"

"Yes." She slowly twirled in water up to her shoulders, turning to face him. "I wish I knew it—like you."

He shrugged. "Grew up here . . . 'til I was ten."

"I wish I knew . . ." She revolved in the water again. "Everything I can see here."

Til stood up and stretched. Then he began ambling along the bank, moving slowly around the pond, his hand touching or pointing to every tree, flower, plant.

"Spruces—one, two, three. This is a cedar. There's another. Ash. Here's a big spruce fallen down."

"Why?"

He stopped and turned to her.

"What makes such big trees fall? Lightning?"

"Sometimes—or the ground gets soft, gets too weak to hold it. The wind finishes it. These are all ferns here." The fallen tree bridged one end of the pond, and Til walked across it. "Lots of moss on the trunk and look, in the water, islands of moss. Violets blooming there. More spruce."

Here eyes were following *him* now, not his hand when it brushed a tree or pointed to a plant. She watched him and noted how he moved in a sure, effortless step, an easy grace, an unconscious oneness with everything he saw and touched. She watched a person who belonged somewhere, a man with a place.

"Grasses. These are dying from too much water. The pond'll kill these trees too in time. Be a big clearing here in a few years, maybe someday a meadow." As he ranged around the pond, examining the life there, he forgot his strained feelings with the Widow, even forgot Mag. There was only the

FOREST THINGS

pond and the life around it and the girl inside of it. "Spruce. Spruce. Mossy rocks there. Feel that."

She ran a hand over the silky moss. Her large eyes registered the circle of life around the pond, then rested on Til.

"Your father taught you?"

He nodded.

She stared. "Was he patient with you?"

"Yes," Til said.

She dropped her gaze into the water.

Til's heart cracked and he wanted to touch her, to cup those small, wet shoulders and kiss the top of her head. "You could learn it," he said. "You could learn it circle by circle— the whole forest. Go ahead."

She looked up at him.

He gestured around the pond. "Go on."

She revolved slowly in the water, her face twisted in concentration. "Uhh, spruce. Spruce. Spruce. And . . . cedar." She drew her arm out of the water, her finger pointing as it dripped gems back into the pond. The sun rained sparks all around her. Til watched and was awed by her, proud of her. "Ash tree, ferns . . . grasses. Oh, moss on the trunk and . . . moss in the water. Violets there. Spruce. Spruce. Grass." Her eyes came around to him, questioning.

He smiled his pleasure and his pride. He smiled how much he liked her. Her eyes held. That bit of joy she kept hidden and protected peeked out at him. She smiled and, like her brother, tried to hide it by twisting her mouth.

"See what I mean," Til said. "You're learning it."

Til heard it first and twisted his head like an animal, listening hard. Lyn heard it then. Her name was being called by her brother.

The joy the girl had shown skittered back out of sight. She bit her lip, thinking, then began walking to the edge of the pond.

The faraway voice said, "Lyn!" and Lyn drew in her breath to shout, "Here!" She left the water and went to her clothes

GERALD DI PEGO

and towel, drying herself hurriedly. Hers was a smooth, lean body that thickened and curved a bit at the thighs and buttocks and breasts—delicate breasts, beaded with water, nipples hardened with chill, pushing against the fabric of the suit.

As Allan hurried into the clearing, he saw his sister bending over to slip into her cutoff jeans, saw her breasts nearly revealed, saw her long hair wild and wet against her body—and he saw Til standing nearby. Til smiled and waved at him, but he was too surprised to answer.

"Dad's mad, Lyn."

She piled up her hair within the towel, slipped into her shirt.

"You said you were going to the lake."

"Oh, I know. Let's go."

"Ask your parents something for me."

Both children turned to Til, anxious, wondering.

"See if your family wants to hike up the mountain today, have lunch at the top."

They nodded and rushed off. Lyn turned to wave, and he answered the wave and shouted after them. "Ask the Dermitters too!"

"We'll say we met Til on the way back, and he asked us about the hike."

Allan glanced at her as they walked. "Why?"

"I don't want Dad to know he was there with me."

Allan's look darkened. "Why?"

"Daddy doesn't like him."

FOREST THINGS

"Do you?"

"Yes. Don't you?"

Allan's "yes" stayed trapped in his mind. Jealousy kept it there. Til and Lyn had been together for a secret time, in a secret place, a place of nakedness and near nakedness. It seemed to him that Lyn had stepped away from him, stepped closer to something else, another state of being, something scary to him, something grown-up, something sexual. She had left him behind. "I guess so," he said.

It was a colorful procession with bright orange and blue knapsacks, Lou Chase's yellow baseball cap, Mag's short-legged green jump suit with long socks of green and blue diamonds, Lyn's bright red head scarf, Allan's clean white sweatshirt, Patti Chase's new sneakers with bold stripes of red and white, Michael Dermitter's wide camera strap embroidered like an Indian rug. They sparkled through the green-brown forest as birds fifed and Til Sharkis led the way up Tilima Mountain.

Til showed them berries they could pick and eat on the way, introduced them to the three petrified dragons, great fallen trees that guarded a bog. He gathered them around a plant and asked them to feel it and study it. "Rub it, smell it. Okay now remember that one. It's poison oak." Some of them shrieked. Everyone stepped back from the plant except Lou Chase, who smiled and shook his head. The Dermitters were roaring. The plant was a harmless sugar maple sapling.

He showed them the deep drop-off of the whitestone cliffs and pointed out and named the distant peaks of the Adiron-

GERALD DI PEGO

108

dack chain. He told them some of the old legends and the new stories collecting around Egon Webb.

"They say he can hibernate like a bear; hardly stirs all winter. He also shows up at more than one place at the same time. Hikers have seen him trudging up Mount Tilima, and fishermen have seen him rowing across the lake—same time, same day. So they say he's the spirit of the forest, and he's lived forever. Speaking of bear . . ."

He pointed to a tree with a hunk of bark bitten away, the territorial mark of a bear. "Big one. Could be the black we've seen around the camp. Let's go."

They walked on behind him, more quiet now, eyes searching the forest.

Til turned and walked backward a moment, facing them, gesturing to the side. "That little offshoot trail lead to my cabin, and that means we're halfway to the top." He turned to go forward, but a voice called him back.

"Til."

He knew the voice, Mag's voice. He looked at her, but avoided her eyes as she avoided his. They knew what they would find there. Last night was alive in their eyes, wild and windy and real. It lived in their bodies too, in their fingertips, in their mouths.

She spoke to him from her place in line. "Is it all right if I sit this one out in your cabin?"

Dermitter moaned.

"No, really, I'm tired. I don't want to hold the rest of you back. Just go on and I'll wait in the cabin. Pick me up on the way down—if it's all right with Til."

"We can rest here awhile," Til said.

Dermitter patted her back. "You can make it."

"No, really." She came closer to Til. "If it's okay, I'll take this trail to your cabin. Is it open?"

"Jesus, Mag, where's your energy? Where's all that energy?" her husband said. He was smiling but his words had a sharp and brittle edge. "Spoilsport."

FOREST THINGS

"I'm not spoiling it. You go on." And to Til she said again, "Is it open?"

"I'll open it for you. You people just continue up the trail. It's clear as a highway. I'll catch up with you in a few minutes."

"Are you feeling okay?" Now Michael was concerned.

"I'm just tired," Mag said. "Please go ahead." She took the small trail.

Til followed her. The others hesitated a moment, then walked on.

Til's eyes stroked the backs of her knees above those long socks, moved up to her thighs and lingered there, moved up to her buttocks. He felt himself swelling between the legs. He felt himself smiling, remembering. God, that body had come to him last night, had belonged to him, filled him.

"Oh, it's pretty." They had come to the cabin. It wasn't pretty—unmatched lumber, tar paper on the roof, a windowless front with a slightly uneven door—but it was nearly invisible, so close were the trees, rocks, fallen trunks and wildflowers. The land had never been suddenly and rudely cleared, never cleared at all. Til had built slowly, hardly disturbing the growth.

Mag walked to the door and waited. She smiled, and her eyes brushed over his face, still afraid to stare.

"It's not locked." He pushed the door open.

She stared at him now, surprised. Her smile was gone, and her fear was back, the same fear she had had last night, the fear that had dried her mouth and quickened her heart and made her doubt. This man was a stranger. This door she was opening was a new one. Beyond was wilderness.

He walked in, and she followed. He closed the door and turned to her, his eyes a dark smile. She bit her lip to keep it from trembling, raised her eyes, raised her chin.

"Did I get *you* here," he said, "or did you get *me* here? Do you know the answer to that?"

She shook her head, no.

"The answer is, it doesn't matter. Does it."

GERALD DI PEGO

110

She shook her head again and made herself step closer to him. She took a long breath and felt her fear dissolving as it had dissolved last night, diluted by want and will, finally overwhelmed by must. Her voice was breathy, weak. "The people . . ."

"If they come, I'll kill them and eat them."

Her eyes widened, trying to take him in, know him, solve him, guess his thoughts and understand the moist, black laughter of his look.

He put his fingertips on her temples and slowly pushed them into her hair. She closed her eyes.

"Look at me."

She did. Fear and must.

"Are we crazy?"

She didn't answer. She put her hands over his.

"Are they?"

She took a step, came against him.

He smelled her. He felt her heart beating. She wanted him to begin it. She wanted him now, without time to think, without words. Mute. The Widow wanted him blind. Mag would have him mute. The Widow would take out his eyes. Mag would have his tongue. They would cripple him and keep him.

He could grip this full, tight-bodied woman and squeeze speech from her. He could pick her up and shake words out of her mouth, but he didn't. He forgave her and blessed her and ached to have her. All she wanted was abandon, and that he understood. He used it himself like a drug. In those times when The Memory dug deep into the center of his bones and he could not shake it, he had sought fierce abandon and had found it in drink and destruction, in wild fist fights, in brutal sex, in blood.

He suddenly picked her up under the arms and thrust her back against the wall, thrust himself at her, teeth bared. He took her with anger, his strong hands unzipping, pulling, pushing cloth out of his way, baring shoulders and arms,

FOREST THINGS

111

pushing her clothes down over her rich buttocks, gripping his fingers into that already bruised flesh and sliding them down to touch the moisture between her legs.

She took him with hunger, her legs pumping as she stepped out of her fallen clothes, her fingers working to undo his belt and pants and free his body.

His hand reached inside of her and lifted her, and she caught her breath. The tip of his penis touched her moisture, and he slowly, slowly lowered her, entering her.

She wrapped her legs around him and drew in her breath in a long moan that whispered of death, as if a blade were entering her, as if life were leaving her.

He freed her breasts and placed his mouth upon them. He rocked her against the wall. He cried out. He heard her weeping and laughing. He abandoned himself to her, to it, to the act, to the beast. If her husband should find them now, he *would* kill the man, break him like a stick and bar the door and have this woman and have her and have her and have her.

She pulled his hair to bring his mouth from her breasts. She placed their lips together to muffle her outcries.

He tasted tears. When he was coming he shuddered and held her shoulders and shook her.

She laughed and cried and could not catch her breath.

In a moment they slid down against the wall, rested on their knees, held on to each other. The soft voice outside the cabin exploded inside of them.

"Til?"

It was a woman's voice. Patti Chase.

"Mag?"

She reached the door and knocked limply, just one rap.

Mag leaped from Til's arms and became a blur, reaching, scurrying, aiming feet into leg holes and pulling, twisting.

Til zipped his pants, fastened his belt, speaking now. "We could bar the door."

Mag had no time to even flash him a look. She had rejected her torn bra and was bouncing her gaze around the

GERALD DI PEGO

112

room for a hiding place. She opened the wooden chest, tossed the bra into it, closed it, zipped up her suit and turned to the door.

"Til?" said the voice outside.

Mag turned to him now, eyes wide. He slowly rose and went to the door, shouted through it. "What address are you looking for?" He opened the door on Patti's unsure smile. The woman was leaning away, tenuous, ready to retreat.

"Oh, I wondered . . ." She laughed nervously. "I thought this must be the cabin. I . . . I've decided I can't make it either. To the top."

"Well, come in. Join us."

She came in laughing, shrugging to Mag. "I guess we're not mountaineers. I told them I'd come and find you, and that way the two of us could walk back to the, uhh, resort so you wouldn't have to just sit here alone and wait for us. My legs, gosh, I just . . . It's too steep."

Mag was nodding, still breathing heavily. She sat in a squeaky wooden chair and suddenly put her face in her hands.

Patti stopped abruptly and looked at Til.

"Tired," Til said.

Patti nodded, then studied Mag. "Do you want some water or something?"

Til lifted a plastic water bottle from the floor and filled a coffee cup. He held it before Mag's bowed head. He touched her hair.

She straightened in the chair and took the cup, drank it down and gave it back to him. Their eyes met and held for a moment.

"Thank you."

"My pleasure." He replaced the bottle, went to the door. "Well, I'll get back to the mountain now. Rest as long as you need to. Be comfortable." He left.

Mag rose from the chair slowly and moved to Til's bed. She sat, then lay down.

FOREST THINGS

Patti's eyes moved with her. "I'll stay with you if you need to rest."

Mag closed her eyes.

Patti moved to the bedside. There was a smile in her voice. "I have the feeling—tell me if I'm right. You're pregnant."

Mag smiled.

"Are you?"

Mag stared at her and shook her head, shook it slowly on the pillow, her hair swaying into her face, her mouth parting with the smile, her eyes mocking Patti.

The truth gathered more and more strength and battered harder and harder at the barricade Patti had built against it. The sounds she had heard as she approached the cabin, the fact that Til had stayed behind, the look in their eyes, the feeling in the room, the scent of sex and now Mag's mocking smile came together and shattered the wall and broke through and confronted the woman. She reddened and stepped away from the bed. She found herself at the door. "I'm going down. I'm starting down." She left and closed the door behind her, but it hung unevenly on its hinges and it creaked open again.

Mag continued to move her head from side to side, and she closed her eyes and laughed a low, purring laugh.

The hikers turned their heads one by one, from Dermitter, the last in line, to Lyn, who was leading, each face moving around to look back as though summoned by something in the forest. They identified the sound of footsteps, running steps, approaching with such speed that they all stopped on the trail, their heads still turned, waiting.

GERALD DI PEGO

Til raced into view, caught up with them and raced by without even a look, bringing each face around like a turnstile as he passed.

"What's the hur . . ." Dermitter said, and Allan laughed. Lou Chase made a face, and Lyn ran. She ran as though Til's passing had raised a gust of wind, and the wind had caught her and pulled her along. She ran hard, ten feet behind Til, and disappeared around a bend in the trail. Allan laughed again and began to run too.

"Wait," Chase said, but the boy ran on. He shouted, "Hey!" The word caught Allan like a hook, held him, slowed him to a walk.

Til had run to a ledge of the mountain that widened to a rock-studded clearing. There he stopped, and he danced. He sang without words, sang as a fiddle and a banjo and thumped his boots on the ground and sprang into the air. He danced to Lyn and held out his hands, asking for hers. She slowly raised them. He took her and danced her to the edge of the cliff and back again. He held her out at the length of their connected arms and spun with her, whirling around, their shoes raising a circle of dust.

Outside the circle was Allan, his smile grown faint and forced from being left out; and Michael Dermitter, grinning joyously and behind his grin thinking Til a fool; and Lou Chase feeling his anger growing inside his chest, forming into another shout because the dance was dangerous, because it was wild, because the man held his daughter and whirled her body around.

Lyn was sweating, her heart pounding, hair aloft. She released her joy, smiled it at Til.

He whooped and let her go, dancing stiff-legged, stiff-armed, as he sang, as she clapped for him. He danced to the edge of the mountain and jumped off.

They each sucked in a short breath of mountain air and kept it tight in their chests until they heard him singing and dancing on a lower ledge, five feet below the trail.

FOREST THINGS

Day held out a long time, stingy with each second. The sun was a red ball balanced on the horizon, heavy and hot.

Night, impatient, squeezed the sky, and the ball lost its shape. Flat on top and bottom, it grew longer, thinner, and then it burst, bleeding crimson into the clouds.

Til watched the light turn pink on his clothes, his hands. The day was dead, and now the night would erase all traces. In half a minute the pink was gone. There was no stain.

He rose and went into his cabin, lit a kerosene lamp and sat on the floor near the wooden chest. He drummed gently on the lid a moment, singing softly.

Inside the chest were songbooks, an old banjo and a torn brassiere. Til laughed and laid his head on the lid of the chest. Inside were a boy forever ten years old and a father stuck in time. Inside were a thousand remembered moments of an age when he was not alone, never alone, when he went about day and night full of himself and seeking nothing but adventure. Inside was one dangerous, unmuzzled memory with teeth and claws, The Memory, the image of a day of screaming, night of loss. He had lost his father and most of himself. He had been sent spinning, aimless, wandering and alone, forever alone. He had been alone in a house full of cousins in Utica. He had been alone with school friends, with girls in cars and in fields and in beds. He had been alone in the army and in jail and at work, and he had been drawn back here, back to Tilima, back to the mountain and the cabin and the forest where he had had a life, where he had lost it.

He opened the lid of the chest. He smiled and chose the bra and pulled it out, examined it. It was too light to register on

GERALD DI PEGO
———
116

the scale of his hand. It was almost nothing. He could hide it all in one closed fist. It was nearly transparent. He recalled the breasts it was used to holding. He imagined Mag and sat her before him on the chest.

She had brought the summer storms. His life had been ready, collecting the clouds, signaling with thunder. She had brought the lightning. *She* had, her with the short brown hair and delicate neck. He smiled at her. He had conjured her naked, and she sat with straight back and hands folded in her lap. So innocent, but with her had come the lightning bolts and the raging wind and moments of not being alone. No. That wasn't quite right. What they gave each other was not "not being alone." It was "not being." For a moment, in each other's arms, they didn't exist, life didn't exist, so there could be no searching, no fears, nothing. That was their gift to each other. It was not the opposite of alone, but it was something, a temporary getaway, a transitory loss of mind and soul, a tempting madness.

Mag had disappeared from the edge of the open chest. His father sat there now. Til blinked him away and flexed his shoulders, ducked his head, dodging The Memory and its fears, the ugliest of fears—that here too he was alone, a visitor, inhabiting his father's cabin, living out his father's life like a ghost, haunting the mountain and not living at all, because he did not exist, because he had been lost, because on that day, day of screams, his father had denied him, erased him.

He suddenly slammed the lid down hard, hearing it, feeling it crack. He held it down a moment as if trapping something inside. When he took his hand away, he noticed that the bra was still wound around his fist. He brought it close to his face, smelled the scent of Mag, felt her softness with his fingertips. He stood and went to the lamp, blew it out. He opened the cabin door and stepped outside into the darkening forest.

The Widow Rendon had tried all day to find her dead husband. She had searched for him in every photograph, those

FOREST THINGS
___

framed and familiar, upright on dresser and piano, and those old brittle ones caught in books and lost to her for twenty years. He had lived his whole married life again today in her hands as she had sorted out the images, his hair gray, then black, then gray again as he weaved at random through unconnected time.

She found his image, but not him. The eyes were blurred or vague or looking off or closed. She had not found him in the photos and now, at night, she moved through the lodge, searching for him in the things he had touched and left behind.

His clothes that had not been given away had been taken over by her. She had worn them all these years and he had been slowly washed and faded from them. He was not alive in his tools either, for other hands had used them and marked them since his death.

She searched through the living room with her eyes and her hands, hoping to see him or touch him. She found his old books, three nicely bound classics he had been given, but he had never read them so the books were crisp and cold and gave her nothing.

She found him in his fishing rods in the hall closet. Three rods, taken apart and carefully bound with string, still leaning into a corner where he had leaned them twelve years ago.

She knelt on the floor of the closet among the boots and coats and stared at the rods. She had come to apologize. She had come to try to explain why she had been going to another man's bed, to the bed of Til Sharkis, whom they had both known as a boy. When she drew in her breath to start, the glimmer of life in those fishing rods went out like a match.

The Widow sat and rested her head on her drawn-up knees. Her husband wasn't anywhere. The photos were just paper, the clothes only cloth and the rods were wood and steel and string. She could not find him because he was not alive inside of her. He was gone. He had been gone a long while.

She had meant to apologize, but now she only said good-bye in a long and quaking sigh.

GERALD DI PEGO

Til had climbed a birch tree, one of the sharp slashes of white in the great green and brown forest. He sat on a limb and watched the night sky and, beneath the night, the lake and the lodge and the cabins. It was a fat limb he sat upon, and he was comfortably nestled against the wide tree, one leg dangling down, his eyes on the still-lighted windows of the Widow and the Chases and the Dermitters. In his hands he gently worked and wound the fabric of the torn brassiere. "Mag," he whispered, and his eyes came alight. An owl screeched. A raccoon paused in the thicket. "Mag." The last lighted window went dark in the lodge. Til spoke at full voice. "Mag." The raccoon dashed for safety. A night bird screamed. The Chase cabin went dark. Til stood up on the limb, his eyes laughing darkly. He filled his lungs and he howled.

"Shhhhh!" Dermitter's breath slashed at his wife, silencing her. They both heard the last of the distant howling and turned to each other.

"Banshee," Mag said.

"No, really, what? A wolf?"

"We're not north enough." Mag curled her bare legs under her on the sofa, went back to the book she had been reading

FOREST THINGS

aloud. " 'She searched through her mind the way she would look through her purse, pulling things out, examining them, stuffing them back in. Something important was . . .' "

"Wait a minute." Dermitter had been lying on the bed, still clothed. He went to the window. "What *was* that? Coyote? Dog? Indian?"

"My God, you think they'll attack?"

He stared at the shadow forest a moment, nodding. "Iroquois. They'll attack when the drums stop." He went to the corner of the room where he had leaned the rifle Chase had loaned him. The bolt and ammunition were out of the gun for safety, lying on the floor. He held the rifle in his hands and turned to Mag. "Would you load my guns, tear bandages from your petticoats, stand beside me?"

She lifted her flannel shirt to show her underwear. "Would these do for petticoats?"

"*Would* you?"

"What?"

"Stand beside me?"

"Oh, Michael, put the gun away before you . . ."

"*Would* you?"

She lowered her book into her lap, staring at him now. "No. I wouldn't stand beside you and be your gun loader. I'd get my own gun, or I'd get a kitchen knife and scalp them as they came in. Together we'd wipe out the whole tribe."

He went back to the window, still holding the gun. He liked the weight of it in his hands, the feel of his finger slipping into the trigger guard. He stared out from his cabin and imagined the tall, straight Indians of the North, the glimmer of feathers, the dash of a painted warrior from tree to tree.

Something moved on the edge of his vision, some lighter shadow against the deeper shadow of the woods, something large and quick. Michael's body jerked and the gun butt struck the sill. His voice was hushed with emergency. "I *did* see something."

"Well, don't shoot, for God's sake. The Indians have a bureau in Washington now."

GERALD DI PEGO

120

"I mean it."

There came a growl, a short coughing growl with teeth in it, growl of a beast.

Mag hurried to the window, stretching to look over Michael's shoulder. Living darkness. The night revealed nothing except at the corners of her vision, at the strained limits of her hearing, teasing sights and sounds, never clear, darting, dodging, whispering possibilities. Her eyes chased them. Her ears ached to catch them.

In a moment her focus changed, and she saw the glass, saw the two of them reflected in the pane, saw the watchers watching the night again. She thought of the park and turned away in disgust.

Her eyes brushed around the room, brushed over the far kitchen window, suddenly tripping an alarm that jolted her body and made her scream. There was a face pressed to that glass, barely glimpsed, then gone. The scream was already out of her mouth by the time her brain told her it was Til's face. Til.

She felt hollow, emptied by the shock. She sat on the bed.

Michael was racing across the room. "What?! What did you see!?"

She put her face in her hands and began to laugh. Til was out there, watching them even now, watching her laugh.

"Mag!"

She shook her head.

"Goddamnit! What?!"

She looked up, her face moist with laughter. "Nothing."

"Nothing! Jesus! You screamed!"

"Just a joke."

"Oh, for Christ's sake."

"Well, look at you. You need a joke."

He shot her an ugly, angry look and went back to the window, his hands tight on the rifle.

She remained on the bed, sitting up on her legs, smiling at the night, for she knew it now. She had seen its face.

FOREST THINGS

"Hear it?" Michael slapped at the wall switch. The cabin was now dark but for a small bedside lamp. He whispered. "Listen."

She let her hands drop to her bare thighs. She felt her flesh, and she spoke his name silently inside her mouth. Til. She was giddy with her secret, proud. The night had come howling and prowling for *her*, watching and wanting *her*. What would it do? She unbuttoned her shirt, left it on, teasing the living blackness at the window.

The night growled a deep, throaty growl just outside the cabin.

Dermitter jumped back a full step.

Mag rose up on her knees, held her breath.

A body brushed the cabin wall.

Dermitter charged to the ·corner of the room where the ammunition lay. He was whispering, "Son of a bitch, son of a bitch," and he was trembling as he swept up the bullets and the bolt and rushed to the bed. He sat in the lamplight and hurriedly loaded the rifle.

"Michael, don't."

"Are you crazy!"

"Don't load it. It scares me."

"And the bear doesn't?"

"No. The bear's outside. What do you think he'll do—try to come in?"

He answered her with his hands, pressing the heavy bullets into the clip, fitting the bolt and closing it with two sharp clicks. He went to the kitchen window and stared at the back of the lodge, at the bare bulb there and the circle of light it spread on the grass and threw into the air.

The rifle was much heavier now that it was loaded. It filled his hands with power, dragged down on his arms with the weight of a deadly, serious force. His finger slipped into the trigger guard, and he was ready. Let them come—with faces and chests painted, with arrows and warclubs. He held in his hands a thing of wood and steel and lead and powder, a

GERALD DI PEGO

clicking, snapping machine he could raise to his shoulder, cradle against his cheek and release. He could tear the night apart and kill whatever was hiding inside of it.

He wished it would happen. He longed for it all to be reduced to that simple and terrible moment of rifle and cabin and Indians—his wife behind him, his life on the line. He would kill the Iroquois or they would kill him—life reduced to the certainty and simplicity of wood, steel, lead and powder. Let them come.

"All he has to do," Michael said, "is walk into that light."

"And you'd shoot him."

"Yes."

"Man shoots black bear from cabin window. Fine—two thousand dollars."

"He's a dangerous animal. He smashed our porch. Chase said they'll probably put a bounty on him."

"Mike Dermitter—bounty hunter. Soldier of fortune. Bear killer."

He searched the ragged edges of the light, his hands on the rifle turning white. Why wasn't she behind him? How could she mock him? How could she smile? Didn't she sense the danger? Didn't she fear the Iroquois?

He turned to her, about to speak, but saw how very far away she was, kneeling on the bed in the dim orange lamplight and slipping out of her shirt, bare breasted, eyes wet with laughter, lips parted. He stepped toward her, his voice low and choked.

"I suppose it doesn't bother you at all, right? You're not a bit afraid. You're just going to bed now. Not a thought."

"I'm not going to bed. I'm going to see what happens. I can't wait to see what happens."

There was a bright dot of lamplight in each of her eyes, signaling humor, challenge, the same challenge she had thrown him last night, sitting astride him, goading him. He could swing the rifle butt now and put out those lights, or he could drop the rifle and leap for her and push her down on

FOREST THINGS

———

123

that bed. He could take those breasts, that body. He could have her this minute, and it would not be like last night. He could take her now with great force and fury.

His mind sprang at her, leaving his body behind. He might have torn himself free and followed his imaginary hands with his real ones. He might have actually thrown himself on her, but something happened behind him, something outside the window. He saw it or sensed it and turned quickly. He went cold inside. There was no longer a light burning at the back of the lodge. The darkness was hard and fast now. Black stone.

"It's out!" He whirled on Mag. "The light! *Why are you smiling?!*"

"Mrs. Rendon turned it out."

"She leaves it on all night!"

"All right, the bear turned it out."

He rushed across the room, and she scrambled off the bed, out of his way. He reached for the lamp.

"Leave it on!"

His fingers fumbled for the switch, missed it. He flung the lamp off the bed table, and it crashed on the floor, the bulb exploding, all light dissolving. There was no moon. The cabin was part of the night now, and they stood inside the night and watched each other's shadow, heard each other's breathing.

Outside the beast hurried by, bumping the cabin wall so that it creaked.

In a moment Michael spoke. "I'm going to kill it."

"You can't." She heard him move, his shoes crunching bits of glass. "It won't let you. It won't come walking in and let you."

"I'm going to kill it." He was moving toward the door.

"Michael."

Outside, the woodpile collapsed. Something scratched along the wall. A body struck the cabin, shaking the window glass.

Michael groped ahead of him. The rifle barrel struck the door. He touched the knob.

GERALD DI PEGO
———
124

"Michael, don't."

"He's attacking the cabin."

"Don't kill him."

He turned the knob.

"Don't!"

"Close the door after me."

"No!"

He opened the door and stepped out onto the porch. The night circled him. The back of his neck grew tight and cold. Anywhere. It could be anywhere.

"Michael!" She screamed in a whisper and rushed out the door after him, grabbed for him and caught his shirt. He twisted free of her and pushed her. She stumbled and fell back against the open door. He pitched down the porch steps but kept his balance and ran out to the middle of the treeless yard, where he stopped and turned in a circle, the rifle ready at his hip. He was terrified and he was proud. He had done it. He had gone beyond the wood and the glass. He had come outside where life was—and death. Let it come.

Nothing. He heard Mag whisper his name from the porch. He hissed back at her. "Go inside!" Then he made a circle again, straining to hear, see, smell it. His arms were springs, ready to raise the rifle. His finger was on the trigger, part of the machine. Let it come.

Turning about, he moved closer to the trees. The cabin dissolved in darkness and was gone. He was among the black trunks, hearing only his own breath, his swallowing. He put his back against a tree. In a while, when his heart quieted and he had his breath, he would circle the cabin slowly. He would find the beast, a great shadow with teeth and claws. He would fire into that shadow. He would kill the bear, or the bear would kill him. It was certain and simple.

But when his heart slowed and his breath returned, when everything was still inside of him and around him, he didn't move.

FOREST THINGS

Mag stood on the porch, bruised and shivering. A wind had come off the lake and chilled her, a light, tricky wind that made branches click together and dead leaves dance. She snapped her head one way, another. She moved to the porch steps and whispered, "Michael. Please!" The breeze played over her nakedness. She held her upper arms and stepped carefully down the three porch stairs. "Michael!" She moved along the side of the cabin to where she had last heard Til. The darkness was utter, solid. Her stare bounced back from it. The night had a voice that whispered without words. It had fingertips that stroked her flesh, turning her to ice. "Oh, God . . . Til!" she whispered, hoping Michael wouldn't hear. "Til!" Leaves tapped the cabin wall. She started. Somewhere a twig snapped. She began to fear that the night had no name, that Til had come and gone, and out here was a black animal with white curved claws aimed now for her flesh, right now, this second.

She was caught by the hair. Her mouth opened wide, sucking air, and she flailed her arms, struck nothing. She was held from above, a powerful grip, a man's hand. She held on to that fist and turned to look upward. Til lay on the cabin roof. He released her hair and took hold of her wrists. He stood and pulled her up. Her feet left the ground, struck the cabin wall, walked up the wall as he pulled her to him. She was on the roof and suddenly in his arms and quickly, silently, guided downward onto her knees, onto her back. He was on top of her, and the night had a face, black eyes and a smile.

GERALD DI PEGO

Michael Dermitter stood immobile against the tree and listened to the breeze stalking about him, awakening the branches above him and the leaves at his feet. The forest had been still. Now he was surrounded by sounds as soft as moccasins on damp earth. He was no longer sure he could hear them in time. They could be close enough now to spring at him out of the night, screaming, painted faces, tomahawks descending. They could be beside him now, bowstrings taut, arrow tips aimed at his throat. It could come suddenly, silently. If only he could stand in sunlight on a windless day with loaded rifle and wait for the Iroquois.

He knew he should move. The night was creeping too close. He should walk straight ahead until the cabin appeared. He should enter the cabin and bolt the door behind him. His wife would be there waiting. They would hold each other. Sleep would come. Day would come.

He should move, but he was stuck fast against the tree. His fear spread like vines around the trunk, holding him. In the morning there would be only the tree, he thought, the wide trunk shaggy with vines, a rifle leaning against it and never again a word of Michael Dermitter.

The screech of an owl released him. He marched ahead, eyes ahead, rifle thrust before him. He stumbled, but stayed on his feet. He prayed to meet the cabin and not the bear.

The breeze floated beside him, whispering close to his ear, masking other sounds that might be warnings, might signal the swift approach of a massive body. He began to run, but the sound of his running made him deaf to anything else, and

FOREST THINGS

he stopped and walked on, the rifle held up at shoulder height, his finger on the trigger. His chest and arms were shaking now, and his throat was dry. The night laughed in a whisper. A shape loomed on his left. He whirled and nearly fired. It was the cabin, an undefined shadow that took solid form as he approached, growing a porch, offering welcome stairs.

He hurried up the steps with the night clawing at his back. He rushed toward the door, hand outstretched, and found nothing. He paused in the open doorway, amazed.

"Mag?" He stared into the black cube that was the interior of the cabin. He was about to speak his wife's name again, to shout it, when he heard the sound, a heavy scuttling, scratching sound. He gasped and aimed the rifle toward a corner of the darkness. It was inside. It was here. He said, "Mag," but the word was destroyed in his throat. He stepped toward the corner, his arms as rigid as the rifle they held.

The sound came again, above him. He snapped his eyes upward. It was on the roof. It was thrashing and scratching up there, breathing now, growling now. He stepped beneath the sound and raised the rifle as the beast moaned. He closed his eyes and readied his mind, readied his ears for the blast of powder and lead that would tear through the roof and the beast and the night. He felt the trigger move as his finger gripped it. The beast growled and then spoke with Mag's voice and said, "Oh my God!"

Dermitter was locked in midmotion like the half-pulled trigger. He was absolutely still, not a breath or a blink. He was half alive. He was a brain detached from a still and useless body, a brain at work, examining the amazing truth that moved in the darkness above.

GERALD DI PEGO

128

Til held his hand over her mouth to stop her outcries. She closed her eyes and bit the flesh of his palm, wrapped her arms and her legs about him. He closed his teeth on her breast, their mouths exchanging pain for pain and their bodies pleasure for pleasure until both were one.

Slowly, teeth withdrew from flesh, body from body. He lay beside her, his hands stroking her, helping his eyes to see her through the dark.

In a moment, he jumped down softly and reached up for her, caught her and lowered her. He stood her before him and embraced her. They kissed, deep and long. He slid his fingers into the hair between her legs and pulled. She gasped, and he trotted away and dissolved in darkness.

Mag leaned against the cabin wall, getting her breath and her bearings. She hugged her arms across her breasts and walked around to the front of the cabin, pausing there to look about, listen, whisper. "Michael?" She turned and went through the open doorway, closed the door behind her and felt for the wall switch.

He saw her first, for her back was turned to him as she snapped on the light. He saw that she was naked, that her back and buttocks were scratched and streaked with dirt, her hair in a wild tangle.

She felt him before she saw him. She felt his presence in the room before her eyes found him there, sitting on the bed, the rifle across his lap. Two thoughts survived the shock and remained clear in her mind—that his eyes had been wounded by the truth and that his hands were limp on the rifle, far from

FOREST THINGS

the trigger. She felt that he would not shoot her, and she felt she should not stand naked before him. She hurried to the chair where her robe lay. She put on the robe and then sat in the chair, deep in the chair, huddled and bent over and staring at the floor.

"And last night?" Michael said. His voice was high and whiny, like a child close to tears.

She nodded. Then, in a moment, she lifted her head to look at him, waiting for him to say more, but he did not. She spoke for him. "Why, Mag? I don't know." Then, "Yes, I do. Because . . . I want out." Her voice broke on the last word, and she covered her face, thinking, "Now, now it's real." Her new freedom had been a secret thing. Her times with Til had been stolen times, outside the context of her life. Now what she had done was finally real because Michael knew. He knew. She was glad, and she was terrified. It was over, and it would soon begin. Her life had stopped here for a moment, a silent moment, with Michael on the bed and her in the chair. When one of them moved, when one of them spoke, her life would start again and be utterly and forever changed.

"Why didn't you say you wanted out?" Michael sounded eight years old. "You never told me."

She sobbed into her hands.

Til trotted away from Mag, moving as part of the darkness, running straight and sure to the edge of the forest where the trail began. He felt the springiness of his legs and was aware of the muscles of his back. He flexed them and flexed his arms. He felt his power and gloried in it. He jumped and ran on.

GERALD DI PEGO
_____
130

He stopped himself by reaching out and grasping a spruce trunk. He suddenly braced himself and gripped the trunk as if to pull it out of the ground. He pulled, straining, stretching, testing every muscle. He bared his teeth and pretended to tear the roots from the earth. He held the imaginary tree over his head and flung it with all his strength, heard it splash into the lake half a mile away. He laughed then howled then moved back toward the cabins. He was not ready to end this night.

He circled around trees, putting out his hands to feel the bark, letting the low, soft-needled branches brush his hair and scratch his back. He found himself moving toward the Chases' cabin. He would leap on to the roof, he thought, not climb but leap. He would growl and stamp and jump off and circle the cabin like a raging bear. He would shake their house, shake them out of their beds. They would scream like startled crows. They would try to find him with eyes stretched wide with fear, but he would be gone. He would rush to the Widow and speak outside her window with the voice of the owl and the bear and the lion. No one would rest tonight.

He charged the Chases' cabin but slowed when he saw a dim light through the front window. He crept to that window and peered in.

The light came from a tiny bulb, the size of a Christmas light, plugged into a wall socket near the floor beside Allan's bed. Allan had fallen asleep reading a book by that light, for the book was open on the floor with the boy's hand still upon it. Allan lay along the edge of his bed near the light, his face slack and peaceful with sleep.

Til wanted to know the name of the book, and was it alive inside the boy's mind? Was Allan dreaming new pages, and was the dream better than the book?

He followed the glow of the tiny light as it spread and dimmed and barely touched the pillow of Lyn's cot, softly lighting one loose ribbon of red-brown hair, revealing her smooth forehead and cheek and one closed eye. He studied her, his stare as gentle as the faint light. He blessed her. His mind sent a kiss to that closed eye, and the eye opened.

FOREST THINGS

Til stepped back from the window and stood still. He hoped he had gone far enough into the darkness so he was invisible and would not startle her. He saw her rise up on her elbows. A great pile of hair slid down into her face. Sleepily, she pushed it aside. She looked toward Til and saw nothing. She lay down and turned out of the light, settling her body on the cot.

He smiled and shook his head in awe. She had felt his kiss. She had awakened at the touch of his mind. He blessed both children and stepped softly away, moving up the trail to his home.

Lou Chase was up at half light, moving as quietly as he could. He made a sandwich and wrapped it, packed it away with two cans of beer. He gathered his jacket, tackle box and fishing rod and stepped softly between his sleeping children, heading for the front door. Allan stirred in his bed. Chase freed two fingertips to grasp the doorknob and turn it.

The boy whispered, "Dad?"

But Chase eased out the door, pushed the screen away and caught it with his foot, let it close quietly behind him. He breathed in a great draft of damp morning air, forest scents and freedom. He walked to the shore, to the boat that would carry him far around the lake to secret spots and silent coves, to hours of sweet alone.

He had not slept well. His mind had been rushing ahead, going back home, back to work, listing the stops he must make, the customers he must see, the sales he had better close. He fought to hold his mind back. It must not skip over

GERALD DI PEGO

132

these final five days. It must let him live each one slowly and fully.

Lou Chase wished he could fish forever or play the outfield, waiting for the long ball. His hands and his eyes were sure and fast. His arms and legs were strong. Instead, he sold machines and lived with doubt, on the edge of failure, filled with fear. His competition was unethical, his customers disloyal, his bosses unreasonable. Each workday was an enemy to battle, a personal attack to survive. Each night he brought his unspent fury home and spent it there, among the people who could not threaten him or cut his pay or take his job.

His vacations were meant to be different, lived outside his normal life, a separate world where he could live at peace with his family, at peace within himself. Instead, he grew even more nervous, overprotective of his precious twenty-one days, anxious that each one go exactly as planned, becoming desperate as they dwindled to ten, to five.

He was loading the rowboat when he heard the screen door thud. He said, "Shit," under his breath. He had wanted to get away clean.

Allan came across the yard to the pier, a coat over his flapping pajamas, his voice broken and shaken by the morning chill. "Hi. Going out early."

"Yeah." Chase carefully leaned his rod against a seat of the boat. He could hear Allan's teeth chattering.

"Cloudy today."

"Just as well," Chase said.

"Can I come?"

"Well, I'm ready to go."

"I can get dressed in a minute."

He looked at the boy now and saw the raw need in his eyes, the deep want.

"Okay?"

Chase ached to be alone, spend hours alone on the lake, without a word. Five days was too short a time. His work loomed at him. He needed time alone. He deserved it.

FOREST THINGS

The guilt that seeped through this resolve made Chase angry and defensive. His voice came gruff and peevish. "Give me one morning alone, okay?"

"Okay."

Allan turned to walk back to the cabin and Chase's glance followed him a moment, watching the narrow body, hands in pockets and elbows out like wings, pajama legs flapping. "Shit," he said again, then he felt a drop of water on his neck, and he turned to the sky. "No, goddamnit. No." He would have this morning of fishing.

The clouds were multilayered, light and dark, moving steadily, tearing apart and leaving ragged blue holes. "Good." He might stay out the whole day, trying different spots, maybe lunching on a bass he would pull from the lake.

He decided he would pack the burner and fry pan, take butter and salt, plate and fork. He could taste a warm bite of fish, too hot to swallow. He held it in his mouth, in his mind, as he walked to the cabin.

Morning light and morning voices were separating Lyn from sleep, slowly untangling each thread that connected her with the dream. It was only a distant image now, a boat pitching dangerously on the water, a great wind whipping sheets of rain at the huddled figure in the boat. Each wave that rolled beneath the boat was higher than the last. Each time the boat rose and dipped and nearly tipped over.

The sound of the screen door sliced through all remaining strings, and the dream was set adrift, bobbing far out to sea,

GERALD DI PEGO

gone. "Allan?" She rose up on an elbow. Her brother had just entered the cabin, wearing a coat over his pajamas. He sat on his bed. "What's wrong?" The dream had left her frightened.

"He wants to go alone."

"Who?"

"Dad's goin' fishing."

She sat up, blinking at the window light. "Not in the boat. Is he going in the boat?"

"Yeah."

"Isn't it raining?"

"No."

She heard her father springing up the porch steps. He entered quickly, silently at first, then he saw that both of them were awake. He glanced at her and went on, didn't look at Allan. She put out a hand, but he brushed by it.

"Dad."

"What?"

"Please don't take the boat out."

"What?" He was rummaging in the kitchen as noiselessly as possible. Patti was still asleep. He found the small frying pan, grabbed a plate and fork. To hell with the Sterno. He would find firewood on the shore. He wanted to be out of there. He heard Lyn's whisper and ignored it.

"Dad."

He walked out of the kitchen. She stood in front of him, a blanket wrapped about her, her face afraid.

"Please don't take the boat out."

"What're you talking about?"

"I'm afraid. There might be a storm."

He moved past her. "Not today."

"Dad, wait."

He went out and down the porch steps and he heard her following him. He whispered, "Son of a bitch," to himself. They were trying to steal his day, get their hands on it, first Allan, now Lyn. But he would keep it. He would fight to keep it.

FOREST THINGS

"Dad!"

"Goddamnit!" He whirled on her, and she stopped. *"What?!"* She was silent. "What!"

"I . . . dreamed it."

"Oh, for Christ's sake." He went on to the boat, walking fast. She followed, stepping on the blanket, half tripping, her long legs uncovered.

"I dreamed a bad storm, Dad. Look at the clouds."

"Will you get . . . Will you get the hell back in the cabin and cover yourself up! Go on!"

She wrapped the blanket around her but didn't move.

He stepped toward her, his lips tight over his teeth, his mouth barely opening as he spoke. "You won't give me one day's peace, will you?"

"Dad . . . It was a very bad dream."

He took another step toward her, his face close to hers, his eyes mocking her. "You don't dream. You say you dream so that if it comes true, you can feel like you're somebody special, like you're better than everybody else. That's what you feel. That's the look on your face."

She was shaking her head. She whispered, "No, Dad."

"Yes! You think I don't know? Now, go back." He stared at her until she turned and walked slowly toward the cabin. "Son of a bitch," he whispered and went to the boat.

He wrapped the plate and fork in his jacket, stowed the frying pan. He searched under the pier for a container of worms he had left there, found it. The soil inside was still damp and the worms alive. He stowed the container next to his tackle box and stood there slapping his hands clean against his jeans, feeling ready. He reached for the anchor and heard the first giant drops of rain. They splattered on the boat, splashed into the lake, struck his hat, his hands. He looked up and saw the last of the blue holes disappear. Dark, slow, rolling clouds, fat with rain, dimmed the day and turned the lake an icy gray. He clenched his teeth, his hands, his whole body. He raged silently against the rain, the world, life, calendars, clocks, his job, his customers, his children—Lyn.

GERALD DI PEGO

He wrenched his folded jacket from the seat, sending the plate and fork clattering into the bottom of the boat. He put on the jacket and stood waiting. The clouds could blow by.

The rain broke and fell, a hard, relentless rain, drowning his morning. He reached for the container of worms to save them from the downpour, then changed his mind and threw them into the lake. He left tackle box and rod in the boat to rust if they wanted to rust. "I don't give a shit." His throat was tight with anger. He walked to the cabin. "Fucking rain. Fucking dream. Fucking bitch."

He was hating her by the time his hand was on the cabin door. He stepped inside and took off his wet baseball cap, snapped it to shake off the rain. Allan avoided his eyes. Lyn was just coming out of the bathroom, tucking her T-shirt into her shorts. She said nothing, but the rain spoke for her, hammering on the roof and attacking the windows, a million voices reminding him, mocking him.

Her eyes flicked up to meet his as she passed him, a quick glance of apology. He caught her arm. "Happy?" His fingers bit into that flesh, felt bone. Tears filled her eyes as though he were squeezing them from her body. "Happy?"

She stared at him, searching, studying. It was a deep, sad look, an old look. It was the look of Lyn. It was the same look he had seen on her face when she was only three, staring at him across the beaten body of his wife. To Lou Chase it was the look of judgment. He did not know it was his own judgment he saw reflected there, his own guilt. He only knew he could not, would not abide that stare.

He flung her away, a hard and heedless shove that sent her stumbling backward into the kitchen. She fought for balance but fell, her back striking the sharp, ungiving corner of the table.

The wood punched into her flesh, broke the skin and sent a bolt of pain through her that opened her mouth wide, but no sound came. She sat on the floor half under the table, eyes squeezed closed.

"Where're *you* going?!"

She heard Allan's faltering voice. "She's . . ."

"She's not hurt," her father said. "Sit down!"

Lyn inched back against the wall, still tight and trembling with pain. She heard and felt her mother rush into the kitchen.

"What . . . ? Lou, what . . . ?"

"She's not hurt!"

"Lyn?"

Lyn drew up her knees and placed her forehead on them, held back her crying.

"What happened?"

Her father's heavy step shook the kitchen floor. "I get sick, goddamn *sick* of her phony dreams. She . . ." The floor thundered as he neared her. "You think you're goddamn special! You think you're better!" The steps retreated. The bedroom door slammed.

She heard her mother's lowered voice. "What's happened?"

"I don't know. Dad got mad and pushed her away."

She smelled her mother's skin, her hair. She knew the woman was leaning down, close to her. In a moment her mother whispered. "You promised you wouldn't mention your dreaming to him. You promised, Lyn. Now he'll be like that all day. Are you hurt?" Lyn didn't answer. She heard her mother click her tongue, one sharp click of vexation. She raised her head. Her mother had straightened and walked away, disappeared into the living room, but she had left her scent behind, fragrant soap, shampoo. Lyn breathed in what was left of her mother. She saw Allan in the center of the kitchen, not knowing what to do, where to stand or sit. He turned to her with a sorrowful, disgusted look, disappointed, disapproving.

"You know how he gets," he said. "You knew he'd get mad."

She looked at her brother, and he turned away, shook his head, went aimlessly to the kitchen counter. She could hear her mother in the living room, busy with the beds. Allan drummed lightly on the countertop.

GERALD DI PEGO

In a moment Patti bustled back into the room. "Shhh, Allan." She went to the bedroom door. "Lou, I'm starting breakfast." She moved to the sink, snatching a pot off the stove as she passed. She ran water into the pot, glancing at Lyn. "Are you going to sit there?" She put the pot on the stove and turned on the gas. "Allan, set the table."

"Lyn, too,"

"Leave her alone."

The cabin survived the attack of the rain. A million drops spent themselves against wood and glass; still the structure stood. The rain clouds left to regroup. The sky lightened a bit. Mrs. Chase was frying eggs. Allan was slowly setting the table. They did not look at Lyn. Lyn was on the floor where she had fallen, where she had been pushed. Lyn was a reminder that Lou Chase beat his family. This was a fact that neither Patti nor Allan liked to look at. They pushed it away from the front of their minds. So did Lou. Only Lyn carried it. She carried the truth for all of them. It was her look. It was the wound on her back. It was the purple bruise on her arm and on her soul.

Lyn put a hand on the tabletop and held on, pulling herself up. She got to her knees, then slowly rose and left the room. The others did not look at her—Allan begrudgingly setting down forks, Patti busy turning eggs. Lyn walked through the living room to the front door.

When Patti heard Lyn open the front door, she leaned into the kitchen doorway. "Breakfast is almost . . ." She stopped and drew in her breath, turned quickly back to her eggs. She had seen her daughter leaving the cabin, seen the spot of blood that stuck her T-shirt to her back.

Patti turned an egg, but her hand shook. She broke the yolk and began to cry.

FOREST THINGS

The forest was making its own rain, a second rain, a slow and peaceful shower as the trees shook themselves, and the drops fell from branch to branch and spattered on the ground. The forest blacks were wet, jet black, and the greens were glistening. Every leaf and twig was clear and sharp against the soiled sky.

Lyn walked within this second rain, and it cooled her, the drops making tears on her face, wetting her shoulders, easing the pain in her back. She breathed deeply and her breath shuddered, ready for crying. Her small, straight chin was trembling. She left the trail and walked on, her sandals collecting mud and needles and leaves.

She reached the pond. The water was still and welcoming. She began to undress, piling her clothes carefully on top of her sandals to keep them clean and dry.

She walked into the pond, not minding the chill. The water welcomed her legs, caressed her hips, her waist, moving up to touch gently the raw wound on her back.

Now the girl cried out. All strength and anger and resolve gave way to anguish, and she wailed in pain, her wail breaking into soul-deep sobs.

The forest life near the pond took flight and hid at the first outcry. Then, after a moment, tiny heads were raised, tiny eyes watched the girl. The second rain stopped and the forest grew quiet around her—a silent circle of giant trees, their arms spread wide, rain-battered flowers slowly drying, slowly rising, birds hunching on wet limbs, listening—and the girl cried, her hands on her face, then in her hair. She cried and could not stop.

GERALD DI PEGO

The forest drew closer to her—a chipmunk skittering along the fallen trunk and becoming a statue, a wren hopping to the bank of the pond, a beaver peeking from his camouflage and a man parting the branches of a young spruce to stare at her.

She saw Til and covered her face, then her breasts, unable to stop the sobs that wracked her. She turned from him and walked through the water to her clothes.

Her crying had brought Til to the pond. It had touched him like a hand upon his chest, pressing there, making his own breath short, making tears in his own throat, his own eyes. Now the sight of her bruised and torn back turned that hand into a fist clenched tight around his heart. "God . . . God, Lyn." He began walking around the bank, coming toward her.

She was stepping out of the pond, the water down around her thighs. She was turned away from him and crying and shaking her head, her body saying No. No, don't come to me. Don't look at me. But he was coming and she saw him and hurried to her clothes, slipping and stumbling on the muddy bank, half-blinded by her tears. She snatched at her T-shirt and tried to put it on, but her hands wouldn't work, and the sobbing wouldn't stop.

He came and knelt beside her, took the shirt from her hands, stretched it and slipped it over her head. His gesture, his touch, his nearness, broke down her fear and dissolved her shame. She fell against him, clutching for him, her knees slipping in the wet earth, the shirt around her neck, her body naked and muddy and shaken by uncontrollable weeping.

He pulled her to him and held her there, a hand in her hair, a hand moving on her back, rubbing gently, careful to miss the wound. He felt how the great sobs jolted her stomach. He felt her face against his chest, the mouth open, fighting for breath. He felt her grow heavier, unable to support herself. He sat and stretched out his legs to make a lap. He helped her sit beside him and nestle against him. He held her

FOREST THINGS

141

and rocked her and swallowed tears—tears for Lyn and tears for all hurt children. He held them all, held them close and blessed them, held even a ten-year-old Tilly Sharkis, and all of them understood each other's pain, and all of them wept for themselves and each other.

She slowly quieted, sniffing and struggling for control of her voice, her breath. When a word finally came, it was cut into pieces by her crying. "So-or-ry." She let go of him and covered her face, then put a hand between her legs embarrassed again.

He took that hand, brought it up to his face, touched it to his cheek and waited for her eyes. She looked at him only a moment, then moved her free arm down across her breasts. He caught that hand too and brought it to the other side of his face. He kept his eyes on hers. She met them.

"Don't be ashamed," he said. "And don't be sorry."

She stared and studied with her well-deep eyes still brimming. A smile came in pieces to her lips, a small smile, quivering there for one second.

He kissed her two hands and released them. They went to her lap as she sat beside him, looking off now. Then she looked down at her body.

"I'm all muddy."

"Why don't you wash off again." He stood and helped her up. She turned away quickly and stepped into the pond, kept her back to him. His eyes were drawn to the wound, and he felt hate and anger, he felt his muscles tense across his chest and in his arms. If he were standing before Lou Chase this minute, he would fling himself at the man. He would bite his throat and tear out his heart. He would kill him and roast him and dance upon his ashes.

"I know he's your father, but I'd still like to take his eyes."

She walked until the water was up to her waist. "His eyes?"

"And an ear, and his right hand."

She turned to him and saw that beneath his words his hate was real. She looked past him, her eyes far off and desperate. "I wish I . . . I need to live away."

GERALD DI PEGO

142

"How old are you?"

"Sixteen."

"Got anyplace you could go? Relatives?"

She shook her head, then her lips were trembling again and her eyes moist. "I wish I could stay here and learn the forest circle by circle." She put her fingertips to her eyes, but brought them away quickly as something plunked into the water beside her. She looked at Til as if he had thrown something.

He smiled at her quizzical look, at this lovely, sad almost-woman naked in a forest pond and feeling close enough to him now so that there was no shame, only wonder in her large eyes, serious eyes. He smiled, and he wanted to hug her. "Rain," he said.

Another drop plopped into the pond. Others were spattering on trees, on the forest floor, giant drops sent in advance of a new storm. She stepped out of the water, rubbing away what was left of the mud on her knees. She slipped her arms into her shirt, bent down for her panties and shorts.

Now, watching her clothe herself, he suddenly wanted her. He was amazed at the irony. He had held her naked in his arms and felt no sexual desire. Now, with her clothes sliding up and down her body, hiding her body, he was stimulated and feeling a thickening in his groin. He wondered how she would respond—with fear? Pleasure? Was her body ready for a man's hands and lips? He quickly counted the years between their ages. Fifteen. If I touched you that way would you think I was old? Crazy? Old fool of the forest. A big, cold raindrop hit him on the head and made him laugh.

She was strapping on her last sandal, looking at him, wondering.

"Cold shower," he said, moving toward her. "You feel how big these drops are?"

"Yes."

"Come on, I'll walk you back." He walked with palm outstretched, waiting to catch a raindrop. She walked beside him. "Did you ever think," he said, "what if it all came down in

FOREST THINGS

one big drop. I mean one giant drop, big as . . . well, as big as this whole cloudy sky. One drop. All the rain. Splash!" He shook his head, smiling, imagining. "People would be . . . walking around, worrying, y'know, thinking it might rain. All of a sudden—whoosh! Everybody's drenched. It would be like everybody got a bucket of water poured over their heads. A one-drop rain storm."

She giggled, walking beside him.

"Whoosh!"

They laughed together, hurrying to beat the rain. In a moment they were running.

Lou Chase stood on the porch, his hands tight on the railing, his eyes searching lakeshore and forest. Anger and guilt were warring inside of him. His stomach was tight and sour. He hadn't tasted his breakfast. Lyn was gone. Patti had cried. Patti had seen blood on the child's back. Allan was sullen. Patti was in the bedroom, probably crying again. Lyn was gone. His guilt was pushing him off the porch, toward the forest; his anger held him back. She would come back.

She came with the rain, as the storm broke again. She came running and laughing with the rain and the man, Sharkis. Chase's eyes narrowed on them, his face hardening, hands going to his hips. The two of them stopped in the yard, stared and smiled at each other as the rain soaked them. Then Lyn waved and turned and headed for the cabin. Chase's eyes raked her, saw her T-shirt wet and transparent against her breasts. She ran up the steps, and he moved to block the door so she would have to stop, have to look at him.

GERALD DI PEGO

"You missed breakfast."

She did look at him. "I don't care."

He took her arm.

Her small chin rose up. Her eyes dismissed him and his anger, spoke of deeper things, older, bigger feelings. "I don't care," she said again.

He let her go, and she went inside. He was surprised to see Til still standing in the yard, in the rain, staring at him, his presence challenging him. Chase glared at Til, but the man didn't move.

Til's eyes grabbed Lou Chase, grabbed and pulled. Come off the porch, he thought. Come down here.

Be angry at me. Raise a hand to me. Til ached for battle—because he wanted to return, pain for pain, what Lyn had suffered, because he wanted to destroy the evil he saw in Chase as he would slay a dragon, and because, beneath it all, he ached for the release of combat. It was another kind of wine, like Mag, like running down the mountain at night. It was another tempting madness. Come down off your porch. Talk to me. But in a moment Chase broke off the staring and went inside the cabin.

Til sloshed through the rain to the lodge. He entered the kitchen and stood there dripping. The Widow called to him from the hall.

"Sharkis?"

"Yes."

"Dry clothes in your room."

He took off his boots. She stepped into the kitchen to throw

FOREST THINGS

him a towel. He caught it and began drying his face and hair. She was watching him. He looked at her from under the towel, like a bearded Arab.

"Dermitters talked to me this morning," she said.

"Yeah?"

"If the weather breaks, take 'em into town. They're leaving." She stepped back into the hall.

"Leaving?" He followed her. She was on her knees, cleaning out the hall closet. He stood behind her a moment.

"Leaving *now*?"

"If it clears up."

He held the towel around his neck, stood motionless in his wet clothes. Mag was going. He hadn't prepared his mind for it, hadn't yet lived it in his imagination. He felt a surge of panic. He wanted her again. He feared her leaving, yet she had always been leaving. Mag was a thing touched in the dark as it passes, a whisper and then gone. She was a stranger who had stepped out of her life for three brief moments with him, three wild times and that was all. What he really feared was what she would leave behind, the emptiness that they had been able to erase—three wild times.

Why were they leaving now? Did her husband know? Did she tell him? If he knows, Til thought, it will be one hell of a boat ride to town.

"Why don't you run them in," he said.

"That's what I thought, Sharkis."

"What's what you thought?"

She rose and turned to him. "He said it was because of their car and the insurance and all, but it's *you*, isn't it. You and the woman. I saw it on her face the very first minute. A married woman, Sharkis!"

He stared at her and slowly raised his hands, put them on her shoulders. She tried to loose them with angry shrugs but could not. Her eyes went dark, gun-barrel blue, and fired at him, but he didn't blink.

"Sharkis!"

GERALD DI PEGO

146

"What," he said evenly. "What, Edith?"

Perhaps half a dozen people in the world knew Til Sharkis. Edith was one. These people recognized a certain look that would come over the man. The look meant that there was nothing between Til and the doing of something crazy, no logic left, restraint gone, reason hiding. He could break her shoulders now or he could kiss her breathless. His black eyes were brimming with both possibilities.

"Sharkis . . . I just don't want that kind of thing going on here. A married woman."

He stared a moment. "Well, Edith . . . She's leaving." He took his hands away, took his eyes away and turned to go to his room. "And *I'll* take them to town," he said.

By three o'clock the clouds had rolled back to the edges of the sky, breaking off the assault. Their leaders, two white, puffy giants, tall as mountains, sent smaller, darker messengers between them as they pondered. Should they call off the attack, quit the field? The blueness took advantage of the truce and spread immensely. The sun warmed the earth and beckoned the moisture back. It rose, invisible.

Down below, doors and windows opened, people stepped outside. The Dermitters piled loaded suitcases on their cabin porch and glanced anxiously at the lodge. Michael walked to the Chase cabin, carrying the rifle.

"Here comes Mr. Dermitter with your gun." Allan was standing at the screen door.

"I'll get it," Chase said. He stepped out onto his porch with Allan behind him. "Hi."

FOREST THINGS
———
147

"Thanks for the gun." Dermitter handed him the rifle and turned, eager to be away.

"You're leaving?"

"Right." Dermitter was already jogging back to his cabin.

"Can I clean it, Dad?"

"He never fired it. Doesn't need cleaning."

"I'll put it away for you."

"I'll take care of it."

Patti joined them on the porch.

"They're leaving," Chase said.

"They were supposed to stay two weeks. They *said* so when Til and I brought 'em in the boat." Allan was shaking his head. "So they stay a few days."

"You know *why*," Patti said with great meaning, looking at her husband. She had told him of Til and Mag in Til's cabin.

"Why?" Allan said.

"Never mind."

Lyn came outside and stepped up on the porch rail, stood there a moment, then jumped down into the deep, moist grass.

"Don't get all wet again," her mother said.

Lyn noticed the luggage on the Dermitters' porch. "They're leaving?"

"Shhhh."

She turned to her mother, questioning.

"It's because of Til Sharkis," Chase said. His family turned to him, Patti's look admonishing.

"Lou."

But Chase went on, his eyes small on Lyn. "He chases every woman he sees."

"Mrs. Dermitter?" Allan said.

"Everybody." Chase watched his daughter's eyes. He saw only wonder there, a serious, studious look as she examined the information and weighed the evidence. She turned and walked to the lake.

GERALD DI PEGO
———
148

Til stepped out of the lodge and saw the luggage on the Dermitters' porch. Might as well begin this, he thought. He walked to the cabin, went heavily up the stairs. Dermitter's face appeared at the screen door, a sad-eyed face with a look Til had seen before. He had seen it at wakes, funerals—the stunned, punched look of the grieving. Someone, something had died.

"I'll put these in the boat." Til grabbed the three largest cases. Dermitter nodded. Til waited a moment for Mag to appear. She did not. He carried the cases to the boat and began loading. When he looked up, he saw Michael and Mag coming with the last of the luggage.

He stowed the cases, glancing at the Dermitters' faces but not catching their eyes. They spoke to each other in muffled words he could not hear.

Michael sat in the bow, his sloping back to Mag and Til. Mag sat just behind him, watching him at first, then turning to Til.

He opened his hands, questioning her with a gesture. She closed her eyes, shook her head. Someone, something had died, and she was grieving too. He started the motor. It muttered softly a while, inching them into deeper water, then it roared.

He saw Mag nod toward the shore and he followed her look. He saw Lyn standing on a large boulder, waving, calling out. He waved back, but she kept on as if signaling. She pointed to the sky. Til looked above. The clouds had stationed a few gray guards and left the field to the blue. He waved

FOREST THINGS

again to Lyn, puzzled. Then he turned away, steering the boat toward Tilima.

He began saying good-bye to Mag's body, all he had known of her. He watched it as it sat on the boat seat, as the wind struck its clothing and mussed its hair. It was a good, exciting body. It had given him great pleasure that he hoped he had matched. It had loved him, and he had loved it in return. He loved it still. He wished he could say good-bye to its eyes. He stretched out his leg and struck the seat with his boot. The face turned to him. The eyes struggled toward a sad smile. They looked at him more softly, deeply, than they had ever looked. They revealed the woman inside the body, a stranger who had wanted him without thought, without words, mute. It was fitting that they should say good-bye silently.

The man in the bow stared ahead into the wind. The woman looked off to the side, across the lake and beyond it, beyond the trees and sky into her own thoughts. The man at the motor watched them both and for once was glad of the screaming sound of the outboard.

When Til docked the boat, the Berger brothers were on the pier. They helped with the luggage and gawked at Mag, leered and winked behind her back to Til. Til only nodded a thank you and turned to the Dermitters.

"You go on to the drugstore, which is the bus stop. You've got . . . forty minutes. I'll borrow a car and bring the luggage." They nodded and said muffled words to each other and walked away.

"Christ, what a piece," Tom Berger said.

GERALD DI PEGO
150

Jess Berger laughed and punched Til's arm. "You get into that?"

"Jess?" Til spoke without looking at them.

"What?"

"Did Chet Tumio and his wife go to Japan?"

"Yep."

Til borrowed Dan Clover's pickup and brought the suitcases to the drugstore, lined them up outside where a teenage couple also stood waiting for the bus. The Dermitters had been in the store. They came out to stand by their luggage.

Now, at the final parting, Til believed Dermitter would say something to him, something he had been saving to fling at him, an exit speech, a curse. But the man said nothing, never looked at him. Mag, who jerked her head about and touched her lips, seemed about to cry. Til wanted to hug her good-bye. He hugged her with a look and blessed her. He got into the pickup and drove away.

"Back already?"

"Thanks for the truck, Dan.'"

"Put it down, Sharkis."

"Rest your laurels."

"Hungry?"

"Emma . . . if I was hungry, would I come in here?"

She chirped, skinny wings fluttering over her grill. "Cheeseburgers?"

"One." Til went to a booth where he could stretch out and lean back and brood. "Lots of lettuce."

"Turnin' into a rabbit, Sharkis." Emma crossed the diner in

FOREST THINGS

her jagged step, broken motion, bringing him coffee. "How about that rain?"

"Wet."

"Sharkis, you got a new lady friend?"

"No, Emma, I'm giving it up."

"That'll be the day. Sorry Susan ain't here. She's a looker. Oh, you saw her. Ain't she?" She went back to her grill. Til stretched and put his feet up. Dan came to his table and gave a secretive look about. There were only two customers besides Til, a woman and her young son at the counter. Dan pulled a pint bottle of whiskey out of his quilted hunter's vest. He poured a bit into Til's coffee and winked, hid the bottle in his vest. Til smiled and raised the cup, toasted the man, sipped.

"Thanks."

"Warm your gizzard."

"Mmm."

"How 'bout that rain?" Dan pointed above. "Look at that." There was a dark stain on the ceiling where water had come through. "Came in all morning; filled two buckets. Give me a hand, Sharkis. We'll go up on the roof and take a look."

"You'll break your neck," Emma said.

"I'll get up there after I eat."

"Appreciate it." Dan tapped his vest, his eyebrows arching, asking. More?

Til sipped and shook his head. "Just right, Dan."

Til ate his cheeseburger, finished his whiskey-coffee and brooded awhile. There was an empty spot in this day, something skipped over, left out. He had found Lyn in the pond and held her in his arms, seen her battered

GERALD DI PEGO
———
152

back, but he had not done battle with her father. That was it. He had used his love today, but not his hate. The Widow had not battled him either, and Mag had left his life without a word, her husband not even offering Til his anger.

Til's arms rested on the table like unused weapons, heavy and lifeless. He wanted to make fists and attack. Lou Chase would do. Michael Dermitter? Lex Sharkis. Ah, yes, of course. Sharkis. He was behind it all as usual—man of mischief, drinker, banjo man, runner, storyteller, gambler, friend and father and abandoner. Til wanted to hug his father and then punch him for running away.

He rubbed his face. The whiskey was bringing on memories and melancholy. He had better get a ladder and go do battle with Dan Clover's roof.

"Where's your ladder?"

"Sit down, Sharkis. It's drizzlin' again."

Drizzle gave way to downpour, a straight-down, all-out, businesslike rain that battered the roof and found the leak, soaked the ceiling and dripped on the floor.

"Emma . . . bucket."

"Shhhhit."

The sky went nearly to night. The last of the customers ducked and ran, leaving only Til and the Clovers. Dan poured whiskey-coffee all around.

When a man entered the diner, coming through the wall of water so slowly and unaffected, the Clovers were caught open-mouthed and silent. The man was Egon Webb, thoroughly soaked, hat to boots. He walked to a table and sat. He removed his hat but did not shake it. He did not wipe the rain from his face or hands. He made no move at all that acknowledged the storm. He sat and stared at his hat on the table, drops falling from his beard and nose, from his torn jacket and patched trousers. A puddle was spreading on the floor beneath him.

Dan and Emma stared a moment before beginning the chorus.

"Well, lookit Egon there."

FOREST THINGS

153

"How 'bout that rain?"

"Take a load off."

"Want a towel?"

"Coffee?"

At the word coffee, he raised his eyes to Emma and nodded. When she brought the cup, she asked again about a towel. He shook his head.

"Eatin' anything today?"

"No," he said.

Dan poured a shot of whiskey into Egon's cup. The old man looked up at Dan and nodded once, a sparse gesture that spoke whole sentences—thank you. Yes, that was the right thing to do. You are a good man. I accept.

"Warm your gizzard," Dan said.

The old man sipped, and his eyes found Til in the booth. Til raised his own cup a few inches in a toast of greeting. Egon nodded to him.

The door crashed open and the Berger brothers charged through, blowing and cursing. They slammed the door and began shaking rain from their fingers, from their clothes.

"Well, lookit you two."

"How 'bout that rain?"

"Won't sell any bait today."

"Got any fishermen caught in that storm?"

Tom Berger stomped to the counter. "Whew! Let's have some towels, Emma." He took one and tossed one to his brother, Jess, began rubbing his face and hair. The Bergers were big, beefy men with round, smooth faces that reddened quickly at any effort. Tom came out of the towel wild-haired and crimson, grinning when he saw Egon. "Jesus. Rain's chasin' all the animals indoors."

Jess took off his jacket and snapped water from it. "Egon, you're makin' a puddle. Look at that. Is that pee? Emma, give 'im some towels."

"Said he didn't want any," Emma said.

"Doesn't need one." Til leaned back in his booth, feet up on the seat.

The Bergers turned to him as they continued to shake and beat the storm from their clothes.

"Looks wet to me, Sharkis."

"Ever see what a bear does in the forest when it rains?"

"What?" The Bergers took seats at the counter.

"Gets all wet," Til said. Emma chirped at that, pouring coffee. "Then when the sun comes out he gets dry."

Next to push through the storm and into the coffee shop were Winston Henderson and his mechanic, Don Bright.

"Well, lookit you."

"How 'bout that rain?" Til said it before Dan could.

"Who's mindin' the station?"

"Fuck it. 'Scuse me, Emma."

" 'Scuse yourself."

They sat, Emma brought coffee and Dan poured whiskey, still being secretive with the bottle though there were no strangers there.

"Next time skip the coffee, Dan." The Bergers had a twin sense of humor and laughed loudly at each other's jokes. "Egon, you talk too damn much. Emma, why don't you patch that leaky ceiling with some of those pancakes of yours. Better than glue."

Henderson was a wet, dark heap, mean-eyed and gruff. "See you got yourself a porter's job now, Sharkis, carrying suitcases around town."

"See you got a good mechanic there, Winston. You can stop begging me to work for you."

"God what a great lookin' piece Sharkis brought in today." Tom Berger outlined Mag's buttocks with his hands and grabbed them. "Mm! What an ass on her."

"She said the same about you, Tom," Til said.

"Did she?"

"Yep. She said, 'Who's that ass on the pier?' " Emma cackled and the mechanic stomped on the floor, his mouth full of coffee. "I said, 'Which one? They're twins.' "

Tom Berger was not good at being teased. His smile was forced. He made threatening gestures with his large fists and naked forearms, only half joking, hostility lurking behind the humor.

Dan Clover opened another bottle of whiskey. The rain fell without pause, without mercy. Emma emptied the bucket and the storm filled it again. Jess Berger tried to engage Egon Webb in a teasing conversation. The old man did not look at him.

Jess was bent over, hands on knees, staring into Egon's face but not catching the eyes. "You deaf? Blind? Asleep? I think he's asleep with his eyes open."

"He's just looking through you."

"Fuck you, Sharkis. He's just crazy. Ain't there a crazy-house in Utica? Want to go make some friends, Egon?"

Tom Berger giggled. The whiskey was telling on the twins. "That's probably where he came from."

Jess leaned on the table, his face close to Egon's. "Where did you come from? Where were you born? Did you have a mother? Ever get laid? What d'you do for fun, Egon?"

"He was born in the forest, a few thousand years ago." Til drained his cup and banged it down on the table. "Leave 'im alone."

Jess shot an angry look at Til. He wrapped his hands around the edges of Egon's table and lifted. He pulled the table away from the old man, left him sitting in his chair, in his puddle.

Tom Berger was giggling again.

Jess put the table down under the water dripping from the ceiling, the drops spattering on the tabletop. He went back to Egon and picked him up, chair and all. His brother's laughter went up an octave. Jess put Egon down at his table, adjusting man, chair and table until the water dripped down on top of Egon's head.

Tom Berger laughed himself off the counter stool, squeezing tears from his eyes. Egon hardly moved, only straightened in his chair so that the water plopped into his lap. He never looked at Jess. He raised his coffee cup, caught a drop of water in it, brought it to his lips for a sip.

GERALD DI PEGO
___
156

Til stood and walked toward Egon. Jess turned to meet him, threatening him with his stance, hands on hips.

Dan Clover rose slightly from his chair, standing half bent. He knew Til better and longer than any of them. He had known his father too. Something was about to happen—something quick and loud. Things would break. There would be blood.

"Boys . . ." Dan said.

Til kicked Egon's table and sent it sliding away. Then he picked up the chair with Egon still in it, still holding his coffee cup. He moved the chair to the table, out of the dripping water. Then he turned to Jess Berger, hoping, tingling for battle.

Jess reddened. "You're an asshole, Sharkis."

Til waited.

"Crazy asshole like him." Berger turned and went back to the counter to sit beside his brother. Dan Clover returned to his chair. Egon sipped the last of his whiskey-coffee.

Til turned to the soggy and silent old man, studied him. He and his clothes were stained and weathered together into something shapeless and brown with narrow, knowing eyes, eyes that could read the sun. He had felt so light in Til's arms. Maybe there were no bones in there, Til thought—only skin and spirit.

He pulled a chair to Egon's table and sat, leaning close to the man, staring and waiting for those eyes to come to him, to read him.

"Egon."

The old man looked at him.

"What do you see?"

The man stared but didn't speak.

"Listen . . ." The whiskey had loosened words from Til he never would have spoken." I've been wondering . . ." He spoke them softly so that the others could not hear. "Is the forest a circle? It's one big circle, isn't it. And you can stand in the center and see and name everything around you, can't you."

FOREST THINGS

157

Egon's eyes seemed to understand, but the man didn't blink or breathe.

Til stared at the table a moment, breaking beads of water under his hand, spreading them. " 'Egon knows the secret,' I used to think. 'He knows the heart of the forest. The center.' " The dull tabletop shined for a moment, slick with rain. Til watched the water disappear. "Now I think Egon *is* the center."

He looked at the old man timidly, like a child. "Remember my father?"

Egon nodded.

"Do you remember how he'd run? Remember? He'd run through the forest. I'd try to keep up." He saw the old man close his eyes. Is he listening or sleeping or dying or remembering? "Egon, he ran so fast . . ." Til was whispering now. "Could he be the wind?"

The old man's eyes opened slightly. He seemed about to speak.

"They're talkin' about breakin' wind," Tom Berger said. He had sneaked to the table to listen. He was standing over Til. When he said that, when he spoke the word "wind," his brother, Jess, began to laugh, and Til Sharkis started to move.

Til shot up, turning, his body striking the table and tipping over his chair, and his hand—the hard and heavy knuckles of his right hand—swinging around to club Tom Berger in the face. It was a backhand slap that jerked the man's head back and smashed his lips against his teeth.

It had been quick and loud. Things had broken. There had been blood. Dan Clover stood half out of his chair again, mouth open, but no words coming. Sharkis was still moving.

Berger's head had just returned from the slap, his eyes still stunned, when Til followed his blow with a punch from his left fist, a short, ugly punch, a crunching jab from the shoulder that hit Berger like a log, hit him on the forehead and sent him back off his heels. He was airborne for part of a second, then down hard, exploding a table and chairs.

GERALD DI PEGO
_____

Jess was running from the counter, rushing on Til like a tackler. Emma screamed, not a scream of shock or fear, a curse. Dan Clover finally found a word in his throat and shouted it, but it was only "Hey!" Mean Winston Henderson was standing up in slow motion. The mechanic sat and gripped his chair. Egon Webb put on his hat.

Jess dived at Til, and the great tangle of heads, trunks and limbs swept tables and chairs off their legs and caved in the bottom half of an old jukebox.

"*Bastards,*" Emma screamed, then she ran for the telephone. Dan Clover tried his "Hey!" once more, and Egon stood and walked slowly out the door.

Til had found Jess's throat and gripped it tightly in his left hand, his fingers going deep. He forced Jess onto his back. The man kicked his arms and legs like a turned-over beetle, sputtering and turning a deep red. Til's right arm was cocked for a blow, waiting for the flailing arms to clear so he could smash his fist into that scarlet balloon and pop it.

"I'm calling the cops! *Bastards!*"

"Hey!"

Tom Berger scrambled up and hurried to help his brother. He kicked hard at Til, catching his shoulder and knocking him off Jess.

Til never stopped moving, rolling off Jess, getting his feet under him, standing and grabbing a chair and lifting it high over his head, bringing it down and smashing it to sticks on the floor. He held one of the chair legs in his hand, shaking it loose from the frame. It was an ugly wooden club now, jagged and menacing, wielded by an arm tight and bulging with power, wielded by a man ready to kill.

There was silence among the men. Emma continued shouting on the phone.

"Yeah! Right now! Yeah! Come on!"

She hung up and turned to see the still circle of men and the man in the center. She saw his eyes, saw death in his look.

FOREST THINGS

"Oh, God, Til," she said, her voice breaking. "Please get out of here."

He moved, and the circle parted. He walked out with his hand still tight around his weapon and his eyes still searching, hungry for a kill.

He stepped beneath the rain and did not bow his head or hunch his shoulders. He sent his body forward in long strides, looking only straight ahead, his boots crunching through the stones of the parking lot, finding the road, marching him to the planks of the pier. He walked the length of the pier and stopped at the tall log pilings at the end. He drew back his jagged weapon and clubbed one of the pilings. The chair leg stung his hand and made no mark on the old, wet wood. He clubbed it again, again. He moved to the next piling and battered it with the chair leg, his palm bleeding now from the blows. He struck each one of the logs, crying out, his angry shouts stolen by the wind, drowned by the rain, but the rage lived in his chest, in his arm, his eyes. He bared his teeth and hammered the dumb, mindless wood until his club split down its whole length. Then he turned and threw the chair leg out into the storm. It smashed a long arc through the raindrops and fell into the lake.

When he turned from the lake he saw Mag at the land's end of the pier. She held a small suitcase, and she watched him.

In a moment he walked to her and saw that she was afraid. He grabbed the lapels of her wet jacket, and she drew her head back, wondering if he would hurt her. He wondered too.

"What do you want?" His hands tightened to fists, squeezing her jacket tight around her. "What do you want with Til Sharkis?"

Her lips and chin were trembling. He couldn't tell tears from rain.

"I left him. I . . ."

"What do you want?"

"I couldn't get on the bus. Please! I couldn't." The suitcase

GERALD DI PEGO

———

160

fell from her grip. She put her hands on his fists and closed her eyes. "I want . . . to go back to my cabin."

She was growing limp, heavy in his hands. He let go and she nearly fell. He walked away from her, went to the boat mooring.

"Now?!" She shouted through the storm. "Now?!"

He unwound the line, jumped into the boat.

"The storm!" She picked up her suitcase and walked to the edge of the pier. "Shouldn't we wait!?"

He looked up at her, and she saw his eyes and was afraid again. Those eyes would welcome a storm, welcome even death.

He went to the motor to fill it and start it. She watched him, then dropped her suitcase into the boat and climbed down from the pier.

They moved through black waters they had sailed before. They bobbed and pitched on foamy waves that had played with them before, teasing them with death, while the rain battered down, shrinking the world into a ten-foot circle. There was no land, no night or day, past or future. They lived a storm they had lived before in the dream of Lyn Chase. Theirs had been the boat she had seen and they were the dark figure, huddled together between raging lake and raging sky.

He carried her to the cabin. Her legs would not move. He opened the screen door with the tip of his boot and swung it wide, then he kicked the main door so hard he tore the lock through the door frame. He stepped into the cabin and laid her on the floor, went to the heater and turned it on full. He snapped on a lamp.

"Going back for the suitcase."

He was gone.

She lay on her back. Her crossed arms slid from her chest and thudded on the floor, trapped inside the soaked jacket, too heavy to lift. The marrow in her bones was now ice, and her limbs had no joints. Everything hurt. She could be on the bus now, next to Michael, warm, dry, going home. But she had stopped and stared at the door of the bus and at Michael's back as he stepped inside, and she had known she could not enter the bus and sit beside him and travel those roads back.

He had looked out the window, wide-eyed with surprise, rubbing the steam away to stare at her. She could only shake her head. The engine started and the bus window slid past her with Michael's face trapped in the glass, watching her. He still lived behind windows. She had chosen to live outside.

Now she lay soaked, chilled and aching on a floor of a cabin, in the forest, in a storm. Somewhere outside was a wild, black-eyed stranger that might love her or hurt her or never come back at all.

It was safer behind the windows. It was warm and dry. She might not be strong enough to live outside. She might die.

But the door opened and closed and the floor shook beneath her. Strong hands undressed her as she moaned in pain. Strong arms carried her naked to the bed and eased her down, covered her with sheet and blanket and spread.

She whispered, "Please stay," and, not knowing if she had been heard, she spoke aloud. "Please stay." She felt a hand, wet and cold as her own, push the hair back from her face. She closed her eyes.

By the time Til returned to wrap her wet hair in a towel, she was asleep.

Til undressed and dried himself, moved slowly, gently into the bed beside her. He cursed his hurting shoulder, but enjoyed the pain in his left hand, remembering Tom Berger falling backward like a tree. He moved close to her, cold flesh to cold flesh. She didn't stir. She lay on her stomach, he on his back. They touched at shoulder, hip and down the length of a leg. He enjoyed the feeling. He would have hours with Mag— for the first time. They would be peaceful together, sleep together, wake together. In the morning, he might find out who she was.

The Widow Rendon's face appeared at her kitchen window at intervals as regular as a revolving searchlight. The glass would empty. There would come sounds of dishes clattering, water running. The face would reappear. Her morning activities were organized between glances across the yard as she watched cabin B for signs of life.

Last night she had been cooking when the sound had come —unbelievable to her—the sputtering of the motorboat in the midst of the storm. She had put the fire down low under the

FOREST THINGS

stew and hurried to the door. She was prepared to watch him walk by the lodge and march up the mountain in the rain, go to his cabin. She would let him go and say nothing. She was also prepared for him to come into her kitchen, wet and cold. She would hand him a robe and say nothing. Later she would offer him the stew. Later still she would offer herself. She had planned it, imagined it and rehearsed it. She would go to his door, her eyes open. She would knock softly on the doorjamb. She would say, "Should I come in?" She would ask only once. But at the front door she had caught her breath and watched life surprise her as it surprises everyone who prepares for two possibilities. There was a third. Mag Dermitter was back. He was carrying her in his arms. He put her inside the cabin, came out for her suitcase, went back in and stayed—stayed with her.

The Widow Rendon forgot the stew, and it burned. She threw it away. She went to bed and did not sleep for a long while. She heard the rain soften to a spray and then stop. She promised herself she would never go to him, never again even think of herself in his arms. She promised herself that in the morning she would fire him and she would evict Mag Dermitter from cabin B.

Til was up, standing naked at the room heater, spreading his jeans there, knowing they would not completely dry, and he would have to slide his legs into the cold wet denim and cross the yard to the lodge for a dry pair. He pulled his soaked boots near the heat, then Mag's jacket and shoes, his shirt. His movements made her stir. He glanced at her, but the morning light was faint, and he saw

GERALD DI PEGO

only her dark hair between blanket and pillow. The towel had come unwrapped and fallen on the floor. "Mag?" She didn't answer. He went back to the clothes.

She was awake, watching him, pretending to be asleep because she was not sure what to say, how to begin this. She was afraid if she spoke now he would come to her and want to make love.

She wanted just to lie there, maybe all day, lie there and think. Michael was gone. She had no home, only things in an apartment in New York. She had a job, but not for another nine days. She had a cabin and a bed and a warm blanket and as long as she stayed beneath that blanket and didn't speak, she would have time to think.

The knocking at the door pinched off her breathing and began a wild hammering in her chest. Life had started again. The world had found out what she had done and was coming for her. You missed the bus, Mag. You cannot do that.

Til shouted from where he stood at the heater. "What?"

"Sharkis?"

The Widow. Mag inched down deeper under the covers.

"What!"

"Come out here."

"Minute." He shook out his jeans and swore, began pulling them on, hopping about. "Mag."

She didn't answer.

He put her suitcase on the bed at her feet. "Here. Your clothes are still wet." He went to the door and opened it, stepped outside and closed it behind him. It swung half open again.

The Widow stood on the cabin porch, arms folded, eyes ice blue. "What happened, Sharkis?"

"Broke that lock. I'll fix it."

"Not the lock. The woman."

"She's inside."

"I know! Where's her husband?"

"He left."

"Lord. So you're taking over where he left off. One day him. Next day you. Lord."

"What d'you want?"

"What do I *want*! I want her out of there."

"Why? She'll rent it again."

"I don't want her rent. I want her out. And you too. You don't work for me anymore."

Mag called from her bed. "Wait. Please!"

The Widow took a breath, staring hard at Til.

"I just need the cabin for a few days," Mag said. "I just need some ti . . ."

"Sharkis, you take her back to town now, and you don't need to come back." The Widow walked from the porch and aimed for the lodge, her arms still folded across her chest.

Til watched her walk away. Then he turned and pushed the broken door all the way open. Mag was still in the bed, sitting up, her head on her drawn-up knees. He went inside, sat on the bed. He didn't know she was crying until she spoke, her voice wet and broken.

"Shit. Christ. Where am I . . . supposed to go? I just . . . I need some time."

"You can get a room in town," Til said. "Or you can come up to my cabin."

The Chase family watched the exodus while pretending not to watch. Lyn and Allan were on the porch steps, staring off at the lake, the sky, stealing swift glances at Til and Mag. Patti Chase and Lou were in the living room, well back from the windows, watching Til with his bundle of clothes, his boots tied together and hung around his neck, watching Mag with her suitcase and uncombed hair, watching them leaving the cabin and walking to where the forest trail began.

Lou was shaking his head, disgusted, making bitter, hissing sounds. Patti looked at him and smiled with a secret excitement. "My God," she said, thinking of the people she would tell: Then they walked up the mountain to live at his place. "Can you believe it?"

"Really dumb," Allan said to Lyn. Til and Mag were too far away to hear. "I mean, she's still married. They don't care, do they."

To the boy, love and sex, marriage and adultery, were mostly mysteries. His ignorance made him defensive and angry, angry at Til for entangling himself in something so dark, something so distant from Allan Chase. He wished he and Til were out in the boat again. Til would explain.

From the looks and whispers of his parents he sensed he was witness to something unclean. The perpetrators were supposedly lower, lesser humans on the moral scale, closer to animals. The victim was Michael Dermitter. "What if her husband finds out?"

"I guess that's why he left," Lyn said. She watched them disappear among the trees and felt sad—for herself because she had only four days left in the forest and now Til would not be part of them, and for Til because Mag Dermitter was not a runner.

Mag saw the cabin with a different eye. The outside was no longer pretty and the inside was damp and cold and smelled of mildew.

"Fire'll help," Til said. He arranged tinder and logs in the fireplace.

FOREST THINGS
———
167

Mag put her suitcase down. It was glaringly new and out of place among Til's things. She slid it into a shadowy corner and wished she could follow it there, hide with it. She sat on the bed, huddled in her still-damp jacket. She watched Til as he knelt by the fire. His bare feet were caked with mud and in the mud were needles and bits of leaves. He seemed to have paws, kneeling there, his back to her, paws or hooves. He knelt and blew and there was smoke and then a crackling flame. He drew back and stood. Her eyes traveled up to meet his.

"Better take the jacket off and hang it here. Sit close to the fire. On this." With his hoof he drew a small soiled rug in front of the fireplace. He went outside.

She heard scratching and scrambling at the woodpile. Her eyes hurriedly bounced over the plank floor, the walls, shelves, fireplace, camp stove, lanterns, chest and the doorway that was filled now as he ducked inside, carrying a heavy log in each hand.

"Come over here." He stacked the logs on the fire.

They hung her jacket from the mantel. She sat as close as she could to the fire, and in a while the heat warmed her flesh and loosened her joints and melted the ice in her bones. They watched the flames and didn't speak. Each was in the company of a stranger, yet each knew the other's body completely, the feel, taste and smell of it. They had shared passion but never peace.

Mag finally spoke. "I'm sorry, but . . . I'm hungry."

"Got some cans here."

They shared a can of soup and some crackers from a tin, nibbled on nuts and raisins as the cabin warmed and dried around them.

"I want to thank you, Til." She was sorry she had used his name. It had sounded so stiff, that tiny word so heavy on her tongue, falling with such a thud between them.

"S'okay."

"Is that your real name?"

GERALD DI PEGO

168

"Yes." He studied her and she looked away. She seemed stunned, he thought, punched and still reeling from the blow. Maybe *he* was too. He still felt last night's whiskey, heavy around the eyes. He still felt the pain and pleasure of combat, and he still felt the talons of The Memory buried deep in his chest, in his skull, in his spirit. He wondered if he would shake it or die—or do both at the same moment. That was you I was banging on last night, old man Sharkis. Those logs were you. Did you feel anything, Dad? The man would be only fifty-one. Not old.

"It's not short for anything?"

"What?"

"Your name."

"For Tilima. The mountain. My father always loved this mountain."

"He died?"

Til shrugged. "Nobody knows. He just left." He squirmed, restless now, but Mag had found a reason for speaking, a subject to chase.

"And your mother?"

"She was long gone before that. Never knew her."

"Did you ever try to find them?"

He chewed and thought, and his eyes went to the window. "Maybe I have. Feels like it sometimes when I'm out there running."

"I mean . . . trace them."

He looked at her.

"I've worked on cases like that. Maybe I could help—if you want to."

He shrugged and stood, went to the door and opened it. "Going to get some sun soon."

She picked up her soup bowl and noticed that it was shaking in her hands. "Where do I . . . ?"

"Some stream water in the bucket there. No. Wait."

She was about to drop the dirty bowl into the bucket of water. He took just a little water and put some in each bowl

FOREST THINGS

169

with a few drops of soap, used a sponge to wash the bowls and threw the soapy water out the door. Mag had been watching his hands. Now she looked at him, suddenly concerned.

"The bathroom?"

He gestured out the door, out among the trees.

"Oh."

Mag walked until the cabin was out of sight. She became chilled again and wished she had brought her jacket. She rubbed her upper arms and looked about for a sheltered, private place. The rain had darkened the forest greens, blackened the tree bark, turned bare footpaths to mud. She stepped carefully toward a close circle of trees. Once inside the circle she checked again in each direction. There was no one of course, yet she felt watched, studied by the forest itself.

The trees dripped on her, droplets of rain they had held all these hours. Life ticked and rustled in the underbrush, crawled beneath her shoes. She wanted a different kind of alone—the alone of dead wooden walls, closed doors, windows with shades, a clean right-angled room.

She unsnapped her jeans and pushed them down, catching her underwear and pushing it down also, baring herself from waist to knees and feeling shamed, spied upon, vulnerable. Each drop of water, flap of birdwing, buzz of insect, jolted her and drew her glance. Fear tightened her stomach, and she began to feel sick. Her urge to relieve herself was gone. She pulled up her clothes and walked back to the cabin.

GERALD DI PEGO

Til held the old banjo in his lap, sitting on the floor.
The lid to the chest was open. He nodded his head
toward it as Mag entered the cabin.

"Can put your clothes in there."

"Thanks." She was grateful for something to do with her
hands, with her mind. She opened her suitcase and pulled out
each piece of clothing, shook it out and refolded it, placed it
in the chest as Til strummed absently on the strings.

"You play all these songs?" She had seen the sheets and
books of music in the chest.

"Some."

"Would you . . . play one now?"

But he stood the banjo against the wall and shrugged. "Just
don't feel like it now."

She continued to put her things away. He watched her a
moment. "You want to talk about it?"

In a moment she shook her head.

"Want to take a walk?"

"No, thanks."

"I am." He stood and went by her to the door, but he
stopped there a moment, staring at her. She was kneeling
beside the chest. He could see her colorful shirts, dresses,
underwear, carefully placed as if in a dresser drawer. He saw
her suddenly very young. He saw her twelve years old, organizing her socks and ribbons and sweaters, placing them
carefully. He leaned down and put his hand to her face,
lightly. He felt her tremble. She looked away. He kissed the
top of her head. "I'll be back soon."

FOREST THINGS
———
171

When he left she continued unpacking awhile, but her hands were unsteady and she felt nauseous. She needed to relieve herself, but she would not go outside. She took off her shoes and pulled back the sheet and blanket of Til's bed. She got in and covered herself and hoped that sleep would take her and protect her from her thoughts.

She used sleep to move the day along, to save her from words and plans and possibilities. She slept and woke and slept again. When she woke it was dark, and she was suddenly frightened.

"Til!" The word leaped easily from her tongue this time.

"Here."

She twisted around in the bed and saw the faintest embers in the fireplace casting the dimmest light on Til's hand and shoulder and the side of his face.

"Is it . . . ? It's night."

"Midnight, almost." He rose and disappeared in darkness.

She felt him sit on the bed. She identified the pop and whisper of bootlaces. He was undressing. He would be beside her soon, and he would want her. She inched to the edge of the bed as far from him as possible. She was sorry she had spoken. She could not pretend sleep now. She felt him sliding in between the sheets. His body touched her bunched and wrinkled clothing. "I don't feel well," she whispered.

He felt her forehead for a fever, found none. He felt the tension in the back of her neck and began to rub there. When she loosened, she gave way to crying, very quietly, and she whispered again.

GERALD DI PEGO

"I'm sorry. I'll be all right tomorrow."

He rubbed her neck and her back, drew the covers up to her ears, kept an arm around her shoulders. Another person had cried in his arms—was it only yesterday morning? Lyn Chase's tears had somehow found their way into his own throat. He thought of her, and imagined it were she lying next to him. The thought struck him like a punch. He missed her. He wished he were with her instead of alone. Perhaps that was where it lived—the opposite of alone—in the deep, deep eyes of a child who would be gone from his life forever in just three days.

Til made a morning fire. When he turned from the fireplace, Mag was sitting up in bed, puffy from sleep, hair stiffened into cowlicks. He smiled at her groggy stare, at her softness. "Fire'll take the bite out of the morning."

She managed a nod. Her clothes were twisted on her body, strangling her. Straightening them, she noticed they smelled of sweat. "Where do you wash?"

"We can take soap and towels and go down to the lake."

She moaned.

"Okay. I'll get water from the stream." He left the door open, for the cabin had kept the night chill, and it was warmer outside.

Mag eased out of bed and stretched, shook her jeans straight on her legs. She took the blanket and went to stand by the fire, wrapping herself like an Indian. She yawned. Her head ached.

All right, she thought, let's start this. Let's begin this life. It

FOREST THINGS
———

was time now. Yes, it would hurt. She was a recent amputee. Michael had been cut from her like a limb. The shock was subsiding; the pain remained—and the panic.

If only she could shower and wash her hair. She needed to be at her best, to feel good about herself. She had to start clean and combed and fortified with coffee. She imagined a fresh sheet of paper, a pencil that still smelled from sharpening, a list. 1. GET OUT OF BED. She had accomplished that. Gratified, she drew a line through it. 2. SHOWER/WASH HAIR. 3. DRINK COFFEE. 4. BEGIN TO THINK.

She heard a sound at the doorway and turned, her eyes, her mind, expecting Til Sharkis. She screamed a short cry and then stepped back, repeating, "Oh! Oh!" The man in the doorway was ancient and ragged, a scribbled shape with no straight lines, with a thousand dangling hairs and threads and a hand stretching toward her that held a line and, drooping from the line, a dead fish. The man's face was gray and shiny with sweat. His eyes were lost, sunken into deep pits carved from his skull. "Oh!" she said, and she trembled.

He slowly lowered the fish to the floor, left it there, turned and disappeared from the doorway.

Mag could not stop her shaking. She swallowed and tried a deep breath. Then she shouted again, smelling smoke and whirling about, realizing it was the blanket. She had stepped too close to the fire.

She dropped the blanket and folded it over on its smouldering edge, pounding it, shouting wordless cries. The smoke choked her.

There were running footsteps outside now, and then Til pausing in the doorway to stare. He came inside, noticing the fish just in time to step over it. He took the blanket from Mag and walked out the door with it, laid it on the ground. It was no longer burning.

He picked up the fish.

"A man . . ."

He went to Mag and helped her stand. She was still shaking. "Startled me."

GERALD DI PEGO

"Who?"

"An old man. He put . . . the fish down."

It was a bass, fresh from the lake, nearly sixteen inches. "Old man?"

"Dirty . . . torn clothes."

"Egon. Relax. It was Egon Webb. I told you about him."

"Startled me. I . . ."

He put the fish in water, came back to her to hold her shoulders until the shaking stopped. He embraced her then and felt her sigh.

"All right now? Just Egon. He was thanking me with the fish. I'll cook it for us. But later." He drew back to look at her. "I want to catch him, talk to him. All right?"

She nodded. He showed her how to work the stove, showed her the coffee and the biscuits. His mind was already out the door, following Egon.

"Be okay now?"

"Yes."

Til ran up the mountain trail. He knew Egon's walk. It was a fast walk for a man so old. He could be another five minutes ahead. He ran, speeding up to spin the ribbon of trail out behind him. He ran to a turn from where he could see the next quarter mile of footpath. Egon was not in sight.

"Egon!"

He looked at the path, still moist from the rain. There were no tracks. He felt angry and ashamed. He had run blindly, like a fool. Egon had not used the trail.

Til retraced his own steps, watching the ground carefully

FOREST THINGS

now. He was almost back to the cabin when he found Egon's footprints in the mud. The angled off the trail into the forest. Til picked up the general direction and ran again.

He winked by the trees, jumped over fallen trunks. He spotted a deer path and went to it, found Egon's tracks upon it and felt good again, sure of his way, sure of his skills. He raced ahead.

He stopped where the path ended. His pace should have brought him even with Egon now.

"Egon Webb!"

He caught his breath at the sound of his own voice splitting the silence of the deep forest. The Memory had pounced. It had him. He was ten again, screaming again. He ran a few steps to shake off the feeling. "Egon!"

He shouted "Egon," but he heard "Dad!," heard it from a younger voice, a strained throat, tears in the word. Dad! Come on! Where are you! Please don't hide anymore! Daddy!

He could not force himself to shout again for Egon. Instead he went to the earth, searched for a sign, even sniffed the air.

He walked a wide circle, found a print, followed the direction and found more. He ran again, but more slowly, watching the ground. He was driven, pushed by his own panic. He would not come out of the forest alone today, not like twenty-one years ago, not this time. He would find the man. They would speak. The old man *was* there, just ahead of him. He would find him.

The chase led him to a place he had never been, a bog he had never penetrated and thought no one else had—too swampy, full of mosquitos. Egon's tracks drew him inside. Mud sucked at his boots. Brown mossy waters rose over his knees. He sloshed about, cursing, searching for a sign.

"Egon!"

He had torn the shout from his chest. There were tears in it. He raged at The Memory, clenching his fists and pushing himself through the bog. "Goddamn you, stop!"

GERALD DI PEGO

His anger carried him to firmer ground but his way was barred by brambles, thick, deep bushes of spikes a full inch long. "You know, don't you. Goddamnit. You know I'm here!" He felt the old man was playing with him, testing him, maybe even watching him. "Egon!" Please don't hide from me now—I'm tired. Dad! It's getting dark! *Please!*

He found a way through the brambles that left him scratched and bleeding. He still carried the wet and slime of the bog on his clothes, but he could run now, up a steep footpath that bore the old man's tracks.

He smelled something. He couldn't identify it yet, but it was getting stronger. His teeth were bared in effort and a fierce smile. He was close. He ran upward, nearly bent to all fours. He recognized the smell now. It was rot. It was death.

The path leveled off under a thick cover of trees that grew flush against the rocky ledges of the mountain. The earth gave way to bare, weathered stone and there were no more tracks to follow. He moved toward the strong scent and came upon the half-rotted carcass of a fawn.

He stood still and studied the animal from ten feet away. The smell was too strong and the dead flesh was moving with a thousand busy scavengers.

He noticed that a hind leg had been broken, from a trap it seemed, and the animal had been partially carved, dressed, as if by a hunter.

He made a wide circle around the corpse, weaving among thick growth, through patches of near darkness where trees blocked the sun.

He arrived at a burial pit. The smell of rot hung again in the air. Near the pit were several rusted and broken traps. Inside were two skeletons only partly covered by shoveled-in dirt—rabbit skeletons, he guessed. An old shovel was stuck blade-down in the soft earth beside the pit. It looked as though it had not been used in months.

He walked by a great crack in the mountain wall, then he stopped and went back to it. It was ten feet high and a foot

FOREST THINGS

and a half at its widest. When he stood close to it, it smelled of Egon Webb.

He eased through the crack and came out the other side into a low cave, actually a dent in the mountainside, hidden and darkened by the great trees and the thick growth of brush and brambles at its mouth.

Before Til's eyes adjusted to the dimness, he thought he saw only garbage, shin-deep across the entire floor of the cave. Then he realized the great, wide pile of filthy clothes and rags at his feet was probably a bed. There were also steel buckets strewn nearby, and tubs, two of them filled with mold-covered berries. The ground was littered with years of refuse; ancient, half-dismantled stoves and lanterns; a great stack of yellowed newspaper; pots and skillets; hand-packed jars of meat and roots; exploded jars, their contents rotting, even now attracting mice who scurried like broken-off bits of shadow, racing out of the darkness and then back in as Till took a step deeper into the cave. The smoke-blackened walls and roof gave the darkness a texture and a smell. He stared through it to another shapeless bundle until his eyes could define its edges and gauge its size and guess that it was the body of Egon Webb.

Til approached quickly, scattering mice and spiders, crunching broken glass. He turned the old man onto his back and saw that he was dead. He put his fingers to the old throat, his ear to the chest, yet he knew. Egon was as dead as the half-rotted deer in the forest, as the fish on the floor of Til's cabin.

Til stood and looked at the body, at the litter surrounding it. Why now, after living a thousand years, why did Egon Webb die today? Til knew the answer, suddenly and surely. It was because Egon was not a thousand years old. He was perhaps eighty, an eighty-year-old hermit of the mountain who could barely climb back to his hole. The last climb had killed him. Maybe he had hurried. Maybe he had sensed or heard Til following and had pushed himself.

"Why was I following *you*? What the hell could you tell

me? Look at you. Look at this place!" Til's voice was rough and cracked with emotion. He blinked away tears as he looked about at Egon's refuge. This was no heart of the forest, no secret center. The old man had found a natural shelter with the forest guarding the door and a hole in the roof to catch his smoke and filter it out somewhere up the mountain —a hiding place.

"Crazy old son of a bitch. God! Egon . . . living in filth, butchering animals . . . rabbits, *fawns* for God's sake!" And growing too weak to bury them, or not caring anymore. Not a spirit of the forest, this old man, but a simple scavenger.

Til suddenly thrust his arms under the body and lifted. It weighed only a hundred pounds or so. He walked to the cave mouth and pushed through the brush holding the body close against him. He followed the worn footpath to the burial pit.

He knelt down at the edge of the pit and let the bundle drop from his grip and fall the four feet to the dirt, lie among the skeletons. He remained kneeling in the mud and staring at the corpse. Tears stung his eyes again.

"Crazy old son of a bitch. Look at those eyes. Half blind. That's why you could do it. A blind man can stare at the sun. Look at you! Dead man! Empty bag of old bones! What did you know? *Nothing!*"

He rose, slipping on the bare, wet earth, went to the shovel and pulled on the handle. The blade was in deep. It resisted. He spread his legs and grabbed with both hands, bared his teeth and pulled, pulled the blade up through layers of soil, through stones and roots and weeds, pulled it free and then plunged it back into the mud to scoop up the first shovelful of soil for Egon's grave.

He stopped just before pitching it in. He stood there, mud-covered, bloodied by brambles, chest heaving from effort and emotion. He stared at the small twisted body, and tears filtered into his throat.

Egon Webb was dead. The old man had brought Til Sharkis a thank-you fish, and then he went home and died.

FOREST THINGS

Egon Webb was lying in a hole in the forest, lying on top of the bones of animals he had fed upon. When he was buried, the forest would begin to feed upon Egon. Growth would cover and hide the burial pit. The body would disappear and leave bones. The bones would leave dust, the dust—nothing.

The old man was not the center of it all, but he was an eternal part of it, and so was Til. They were two men who loved the mountain and chose to live on it and with it. In turn they would both die upon it and give themselves back to it.

He stared a long time at Egon, his body quieting, his mind clearing, emptying of anger. In a moment he tossed the shovel aside.

He gathered fir boughs and dropped them into the pit, threw in fistfuls of black-eyed Susans and fairy lilies, added ferns and grasses and leaves until the body was covered, gone. Then he picked up the shovel once more and leveled the mounds of earth around the pit, filling the hole and smoothing the top of it.

He let the angle of the mountain lead him back, gauging direction by the distant peaks of Marcy and the McIntyre and by the sun which hung more than an hour past noon.

He found deer paths that would have taken him to the main trail and the cabin, but he crossed them, moving down among the trees, and he began to run.

As he ran, he grew lighter, his body springing down the mountain, and as his body lightened, his spirit rose with it. He was chasing nothing, searching for no one. He ran for the running, and he ran faster than his father had ever run, and his heart was bigger, wider than his father's had ever smiled, for he would have a son someday and hold him to his breast and never run away.

He ran to the pond, which had been darkened and widened by the rainstorm, stretching out to encircle trees and make islands of rocks and humps of earth. He took off his boots and socks and plunged in, washing off mud and blood and the smell of death.

GERALD DI PEGO

He walked dripping from the pond to a clearing where the sun blazed. He sat on a fallen trunk and then lay back upon it, eyes closed. The strong rays warmed him, soothed him, began to dry him. He almost slept.

A sound broke through his dozing, a rustling too heavy to be the wind. He sat up and saw the large, one-eared bear lumbering toward the pond.

"Egon's dead," Til said.

The bear grunted with surprise and turned to him, shaking himself, shaking his large head.

"Yes he is. I buried him." Til lay back on the trunk. In a moment he heard the bear move off.

He turned onto his stomach so the sun could touch his back. He laid his head on his arms and would have slept then, but for the scream.

He was up off the tree and running. Ahead of him was the bear loping off in one direction and Allan Chase blurring by in the other.

"Allan!"

The boy fell and rose and ran on toward the trail. He saw his sister there, her eyes wide, staring just behind him where he imagined the bear to be, pounding along just inches from the back of his neck. Then the bear shouted.

"Allan!"

The boy turned and fell again. Til helped him up as Lyn hurried to them.

"Oh. Jesus. Wow." The boy kept glancing about, his mind still running, his eyes still full of black bear. "Shit. Jesus."

"What?!" Lyn said.

"The bear." Til jerked his thumb behind him. "He's running the other way, scared as hell."

Allan laughed in the midst of his fear, his narrow chest still pumping. "He was right in front of me."

"He's a big one."

"He was at Mrs. Rendon's back porch last night."

"They're gonna kill him," Allan said.

FOREST THINGS
___

Til shook his head. "You scared him good. He's halfway to Canada by now. They'll never catch him."

The children smiled, and Lyn studied him. "You've been in the pond."

Til looked at Allan. "Bright sister. Here I am, standing here soaked to the ears . . ."

Allan laughed a loud, nervous laugh.

In a moment Lyn looked at her brother, suddenly embarrassed, speaking softly. "Why don't you go on ahead a minute?"

"No. Not now. Uh-uh. Let's go back to the cabin. I don't want to stay out here now."

"Okay," Lyn said. "You start back. I'll catch up."

Allan looked at her and then at Til. He moved off.

"See you later," Til said, but the boy didn't answer or turn. He began to jog down the trail.

Lyn watched her brother leaving, her neck flushing red. She waited a long time before speaking to Til. "We go to the pond every day."

"Nice place."

She turned to him. "I know every tree there."

He smiled, his grin stretching to reach every part of his face, sketching laugh lines, lighting his eyes. He blessed her. "I'll take you through the whole forest someday. You'll put your hand on every tree, learn them all one by one, and the mosses and ferns, wild flowers, deer's hair, puffballs, bunchberries . . ." His smile drew in and disappeared. Her look went so deep.

"When," she said. "When could we?"

He put a hand to her face, his fingers very light on her cheek, sliding up under her hair. Her eyes never left his. "Tomorrow," he said.

"I have just two days. Then we leave."

"Tomorrow. Meet me here. About noon."

"I'll try to."

He leaned close to kiss her forehead, but she raised up to

GERALD DI PEGO

meet his lips with hers, a quick, simple kiss. They separated, and still her eyes were on him.

He suddenly hugged her to him, closed his eyes and whispered her name. "Lyn Chase." He felt his chest go warm with loving her. He wanted to hold her forever, keep her close. "Listen to me." He went on whispering. "A man died. An old man I knew. Sometime . . . I'll show you where he's buried." She was nodding her head against his chest, holding him as he held her. "Lyn Chase," he said again. He moved his hands on her back. He felt his organ thicken with wanting her, and he stepped back, his hands on her shoulders. She was a child. Only her eyes were old, older than his own.

"Tomorrow," he said.

She nodded again.

He left her and hopped once, beginning his run. She watched him, and after the forest was empty and still again, she called out.

"Shouldn't run barefoot."

"Saw the bear. Whew!"

"Where? Now?" Chase rose from his chair and Patti came hurrying from the kitchen.

"He was right in front of me. Ten feet I bet." Allan was shaking his head, solemn, deep into the drama. "Biggest bear I've ever seen. Even in zoos."

"Where's Lyn?"

"She's okay. She's with her friend."

"Who?"

"Sharkis?" Chase said.

But Allan had flung himself into a chair. He sat limp and still. "Jesus."

"Is she with Sharkis? I told her." Chase went to the door. "Where is she?"

"I came ahead," Allan said.

His mother whispered. "Is she with Til?"

He nodded, not wanting to change the subject. "I saw his claws. Jesus."

Chase left the cabin. He met Lyn on the trail, alone. He stopped as she walked toward him. "I never, *never* want you to be with that Sharkis, not alone. Ever."

She walked by him like a stranger.

"Lyn!"

She went on to the cabin.

The bear hurried away from the Man and the scent of the Man, running until there was no Man left in his vision or his nose, no sound of Man and no sense of him. He moved toward the high peaks where it would be cooler and more peaceful, where he would understand each thing he encountered. On the way, he caught scent of sweetness, berries ripe and rotting. He smelled old flesh too, dead flesh and the scent of Man again. Man had been here and was now gone.

The bear hesitated then moved on, came across a clearing and stopped as suddenly as if a trap had sprung upon him. He rose up and roared, turned to fight, bared his teeth and waved his claws.

Man again. It was more than a scent. It was a sudden

GERALD DI PEGO
———
184

presence. Man stood before him. No. Behind. He turned. He roared again. Man was here, but he could not see him. Man was here now—on this spot. His bear-mind was certain. His ancient bear-soul knew beyond knowing, yet he saw no Man.

He revolved again and again, roaring, searching for the Manlife that filled this space and seemed even to fill his own body, his front paws slashing the air, his hind legs raising dust from loose, newly shoveled earth.

He charged at nothing. He saw only forest and sky. He flailed at emptiness, and then he ran, ran for the high peaks, leaving the Man-life behind him and carrying it with him forever.

Mag stared at the dead bass and wrinkled her lips, held her breath to ward off the smell of it. She picked up the pot that held the fish and carried it outside, left it ten feet from the cabin. She went back in and breathed again and there was the smell, like a fish-ghost, surrounding her.

She washed her hands in the new water Til had brought. She sniffed her fingers and smelled only soap now, but she noticed her hands were still trembling. She took off her shirt and used it as a washcloth, dipping it into the bucket and scrubbing her face, her breasts, under her arms. The water chilled her, and the trembling moved to her back and shoulders, a violent shaking she could not control. She sat close to the fire, but it was nearly out. She went to the chest and put on a fresh shirt, a sweater over that. Still she shook, and now the shivering had a voice, a quivering sound from deep inside her.

FOREST THINGS

She thought of the coffee. She would fill the cabin with its scent. She would gulp it hot and bitter and feel it warm in her chest, in her stomach—but she had used the water for washing, and it was soapy.

She cursed, and her voice was whining and broken by the shivering. "Goddamn, son of a bitch. Fucking, goddamn . . . *Goddamn. Shit!*" Her shouts reached the walls and bounced back and rose to the ceiling, filling the cabin with curses that became screams. "Son of a goddamn *fucking BITCH!*"

She tried soup without water, and it sickened her. She thought she would make a new fire, but her shaking had not stopped and it frightened her. She lay back on the bed and took long breaths. When Til came back she would have coffee, a fire, maybe a walk with him. She would not say no this time, and if he held her, she would not look away.

Her watch read 10:35. She waited for footsteps near the door. She pictured the door swinging open and Til entering. She made the image go back out and enter again, again. Til bounded in, smiling. Til opened the door softly, slowly, and looked at her. Til walked in and went to the fireplace, did not look up until she called to him, then he turned and smiled and approached the bed. Her watch now read 10:38.

Til returned to the cabin at 2:30. As he approached he heard Mag's voice from inside. He wondered who was with her. When he realized she was shouting, cursing, he thought it must be her husband who had come back for her. Then he noticed the cabin door was open wide, and he could see her backed up against the fireplace, half bent over with the effort of shouting, screaming now, sending her screams out through the door—at him.

"Why did you do it! Why did you leave me all day! You bastard! Dumb . . . bastard!"

He stopped in the doorway and stared at her. She had made a fire, and her hands were black with soot. As she shouted at him, she wept, and she wiped her tears with the backs of her hands, keeping her black fingers stretched out like claws.

"How could you do that!"

"Mag, I'm . . ."

"Four hours!"

He stepped close to her and she pushed him away, printing black hands on the front of his shirt.

"You left me alone for . . ."

He tried coming close again and she marked his face with soot. He caught her wrists.

"I thought you were dead! I thought you forgot me! I was sick!"

"Mag, I'm sorry!"

She fought to free her hands. "What was I supposed to do! *What was I supposed to do!*" He was hurting her wrists. "Don't! Let . . ."

FOREST THINGS

He let her go, stepping back, watching her.

She walked to the stove and kicked it, sent the half-eaten soup splashing against the wall and floor. "I was sick. I threw up. I could have died here!" She struck his bed with a sooty fist, then blackened his pillowcase with more blows, finally spending her strength and sitting on the bed, bending her head down. "There's no goddamn bathroom and there's no goddamn water and you leave me alone . . ."

He set the stove upright and then stood staring at her.

"Are you stupid or just mean or what?" She sniffed and wiped her face awkwardly with her wrists.

"I'm sorry. The old ma . . ."

"I want you to get me some water and make me some co . . . coffee and *help me!*"

He stared awhile as she wiped her face on the blanket and then tried to clean her hands. *"Will you!?"*

He didn't move, his own look darkening. Then he picked up the bucket and left the cabin.

"You better come *right back*! *Til!*"

They didn't speak as he made the coffee, and she washed her hands and face. She was drained and embarrassed by her outburst, weary now. When he handed her a mug of coffee, she whispered, "Thanks," and didn't look at him. They sat on the floor, sipping coffee, silent.

Mag stared at a knot on the plank floor and said, "You had a reason?"

"Sure." Til settled his back against the wall. "Does it matter now?"

GERALD DI PEGO

She sighed, and finally looked at him. "I just . . . I don't think I can stay here."

"Where do you want to go?"

"I'll tell Mrs. Rendon I'm sick. Maybe she'll let me . . . just stay long enough to have a shower . . . and rest."

He nodded. "I'll help you down there."

"It's better if you're not there when I ask her."

He agreed. "Can you make it?"

"After this coffee." She looked about. "I'm sorry for the mess."

"I'm sorry you were alone so long."

"It's not so bad when you expect to be alone, but you said . . ." She let it go.

"I'll help you pack." He opened the chest and saw her things were gone.

"I packed while you were gone. I started out for the lodge, but I . . . came back. I think I can face her now."

He walked her to the edge of the forest and watched her march across the yard to the Widow's door. She had a scarf on her head, suitcase in her hand. She was dressed for winter on a mild August afternoon. He watched her walk up the back steps and knock on the door—brave refugee.

There was no surprise in the blue of Widow Rendon's eyes. It was calm blue, like a lake gone to glass. She had seen Mag coming. She opened the door, but made of herself a second door, tall and strong, locked.

"Mrs. Rendon . . . I'm not well."

"You want to go to town now?"

FOREST THINGS

189

"I've been sick. I just . . ."

"There's plenty of day left. I can take you right now."

"I'm not well enough to get in a boat. Please."

"Your cabin is all cleaned out."

"I'll pay. Or just . . . I'll take a room here. I need . . . to get my strength back."

The Widow moved only her eyes, searching the yard behind Mag. "Where is he?"

"At his cabin."

The eyes gave up the search and settled again on Mag, examining her roughly. "Some of the men are coming from town tomorrow to hunt the bear. You can go back with them. Your cabin's not locked."

"Thank you."

Til entered his cabin, weary to the soul. He shuffled toward the bed but was halted by the wide-open lid of the chest. It drew him, sucked at him like a mouth. He went to it and gave it his hand. It gave him a banjo.

He sat on the floor and cradled the instrument against him. It hummed slow, soft melodies in his hands. His fingers dabbled in several songs and settled on "Shenandoah."

He closed his eyes and thought of his father picking over these same notes, and before his father other men, and far back maybe a Scot or Englishman finding them on a dulcimer —old, old notes belonging to no man and no time, eternal, connected now to Til Sharkis through banjo strings and fingers.

He hummed along, drifting back centuries and drifting

GERALD DI PEGO

190

forward again, and not once did The Memory grow claws and snatch at him. Perhaps it never would. Perhaps he had buried it with the flowers and the fir boughs and the old man.

Close to midnight, Til was asleep in his cabin and running on silent shoes through Lyn Chase's dream. She was close behind him, catching up. The leaves and needles he kicked into the air were still flying as she ran through them, her fingertips only an inch from his bare, powerful back.

When she touched him, he turned to her, and he smiled— but he was smiling through blood, a thick, dark stream that covered one side of his face from forehead to chin, closing one eye, oozing into the corner of his smile, darkening his beard and dripping from it.

She cried out and woke with the shout still resonating in her chest, setting off her heart like a jangling alarm. Allan stirred. She heard sounds from her parents' room, but then nothing, only her own quick breath.

A warm morning wind was scrubbing the sky bright blue, cleaning away even those traces of clouds that hung in the corners and stuck to the horizon. Til was up early and singing, washing his cabin floor where spilled soup had turned to glue.

FOREST THINGS

The wind hid the sound of footsteps and the scattering of birds so that Til's first clue of a visitor was a knock on the cabin door—just as if he had lived on a busy street. He imagined that he would open the door and see traffic and houses, maybe a paperboy, postman, poll taker.

It was Lyn Chase.

"Well, hi. Come in."

"I just . . . I have to get back."

He laughed. "Right. Never overstay."

A smile flickered, didn't catch. "I just wanted to tell you that the men are coming to hunt the bear today, and I . . . I wanted to warn you so you're not in the forest when they're shooting."

"Thank you."

She took a deep breath. "I had a bad dream."

"About me?"

She nodded.

"Come in a minute." He stepped back from the door.

Only her eyes came in—one quick look. "You play the banjo?"

He had left it lying on top of the chest.

"Yes. Come on in."

She shook her head. "I better go. I'll try to meet you at noon. But if the men are hunting . . ."

He came to her, not listening, just watching that face so beautiful with concern for him, with caring that could push through her shyness. He moved slowly so as not to frighten her. He embraced her, and she came against him. He felt her hands touch lightly on his back and rest there.

They breathed together. He acknowledged again his love and his desire for this girl.

"Sixteen?"

She whispered, "Yes."

"Then how come I love you like a woman?"

He felt her breath catch. He slid his fingers up under her long hair and gently pulled her head back from his chest, stared at her. Her eyes were storming, searching his face.

GERALD DI PEGO
————
192

"I'll be seventeen next month."

He laughed aloud and ended his laughter with a kiss to her lips, his hands still in her hair. It was a long kiss, and she was kissing too. When it ended, they stared with wonder for a moment.

She took a step away, whispered, "I better go back."

He nodded, then turned to snatch up the banjo. "I'll play you down the mountain." He held the neck of the instrument and flipped the head to his chest. Even before it settled there, notes were popping like corn, joyful, dancing notes.

Amazed, she studied his blurring fingers, then brought her eyes up to his face and smiled and flushed red. "I love you too." She ran, carrying her smile down the trail.

He sent the notes after her.

His boot stomped a rhythm on the plank floor, and out of his hands came music, filling the cabin up to the chimney and through the chimney to the sky. The happy notes tumbled over the trees and found the girl and connected her to the banjo and to the man.

She laughed aloud, running, the notes in her ears, caught in her hair, stuffed in her pockets. She loved a man and he loved her. He was a man with a child's heart, and in her child's body was the heart of a woman. Man, woman and children—they were connected now by love and need and a banjo break-away.

Mag had had two showers, a meal and ten hours' sleep. It was morning. The sun was master of the sky. The wind was warm. She could begin now. She took stock.

FOREST THINGS

I'm separated. I'm twenty-nine. I'm in upstate New York in a cabin by a lake on a glorious day. One mile up the mountain is a man I have made good love with.

She should be with him now, celebrating this beginning in his arms. She wanted him again and was glad. The weakness was gone. The panic had passed. She should spend her last days here with him, making love in the grass, on the roof, on top of the mountain, in the sky. She would waste no more days. Til was not a coincidence. He was a bridge, placed there so she could cross over from old life to new. She would linger on the bridge awhile. She would make him want her again, make it happen again, the wildness.

She dressed eagerly and opened the door, checking for signs of the Widow, giggling inside herself like a truant schoolgirl. She walked down from her porch and headed for the mountain trail.

By the time she was halfway up, Til was already with her. She felt his strong arms, playful hands upon her, heard his laugh. She charged up the mountain with his image at her side.

She stopped to listen. Music. Her mouth opened in surprise and emitted a laugh. The banjo. He was making music—her mountain man. She would rush to him. He would play the banjo and then they would play each other. Days would pass. My life—she would tell people—was changed forever by a banjo-playing man of the New York mountains.

The wind was behind her. She raced to the music, following the winding trail among the trees and along the clifftops.

She rounded a turn and stopped still. Coming toward her was the girl, Lyn Chase, running very fast, joyous, coming down the trail from the cabin of Til Sharkis, smiling as if the banjo played for her.

A realization struck Mag like a bullet and crushed her heart. Life had been dancing in a mountain cabin, and she had been locked outside. She was still locked out, still on the wrong side of the window.

GERALD DI PEGO

Mag lunged forward, shouting a word that came from her stomach, her loins, not her brain, a mindless "No!" as she put out her hands to stop the girl.

Lyn's eyes had been on the path. She heard a shout and saw someone flying at her, carried by the wind, a wild-eyed creature with claws. She screamed and tried to stop, couldn't, tried to escape by stepping around the creature, lost her footing and pitched over the edge of Whitestone Cliff.

The girl fell silently.

The woman became stone. Only her hair moved in the wind. When, in a moment, she inched her body to the cliff edge and looked down, she saw nothing, no one. She inched backward, stood in the middle of the trail. The banjo played on, uncaring. The wind blew, and the trees moved, indifferent. Mag's hands took sudden flight and settled in her hair. She cried out, but no one heard and nothing stopped.

Her hands fluttered down to cover her mouth, and she began to walk away, away from the mountain and the music.

When she reached the resort, she was moaning into her hands with each breath, moaning just to make a sound, to fill her brain and keep away the thought that followed her like a bat, diving close to her head, screaming at her. She hurried to her cabin.

There were men in the yard. She noticed Chase. *Her father*, the bat screamed. The men had guns. Allan was there. *Her brother*.

Allan turned from the men and shouted, "Lyn!" He stepped toward the lake. "Lyn!"

"Go get her," Chase said.

Mag entered her cabin and closed the door, but not quickly enough. The bat was inside with her.

FOREST THINGS
———

The girl fell through three hundred feet of August air, dropping like a tear from the bare face of Whitestone Cliff. On a ledge near the base were three balsam firs who stretched out their branches but could not catch her. It was left to the great white pine.

It was an ancient tree, doomed on a slowly eroding ledge near the cliff base, but it was tall and lush with boughs and springy branches. It sensed the approach of the girl, and it felt her alarm. It readied and waited, trembling.

The girl struck, falling fast, whipping through the top branches like a stone. The soft boughs guided her. She missed the thick limbs that would have broken her bones. She fell through fifty feet of tree, dropping from branch to branch, more slowly now, lowered gently from one arm of the great pine to the next until she dropped onto the rocky ledge, unconscious, scratched, alive.

The weight of her body nearly carried her off the sloping ledge. She slid, stopped, slid again. Below her was a drop of sixty feet to the dumb and merciless boulders. She slid and stopped again, almost at the edge, with barely enough slant of rock to hold her body.

The pine watched from above. It had done all that it could. It was up to the mountain now, but the mountain slipped from beneath the girl in tiny landslides of pebbles and dust. The wind tried to help, pressing the girl against the rock, but her weight was too much and she slipped another inch.

GERALD DI PEGO

196

"Lyn!"

"Don't call her anymore."

"Why?"

"Don't call her. Which way now—straight?"

"Yes." Allan hurried ahead.

"We walk."

Allan walked on, leading his father to the pond. The man wanted to surprise her, Allan realized. He wanted to "catch" Lyn with Til Sharkis. The boy was afraid and sorry he had mentioned the swimming place. He noticed his father's grip on the deer rifle.

"She's probably just swimming there, Dad."

"Shhhh."

It was the same as when they had gone hunting. Chase was crouched low, walking quietly, his eyes burning a path ahead of them, his hands ready to click off the safety—raise the rifle—sight and fire.

Would he shoot to frighten Til? To hurt him? Not to kill. He wouldn't kill the man, Allan was telling himself as he hurried up the rise of land, making much more noise than he had to.

Chase whispered through his teeth, "Damnit, Allan!"

But the pond was empty, deserted. Allan sighed. Chase's hands went white around the rifle, and he cursed under his breath.

They went back to the trail where the deputy, Stan Willis, and the hunter, Winston Henderson, waited for them.

"I'll go up the trail and find her," Chase said.

FOREST THINGS

197

"We'll all go up. Might as well start from there." Willis began to walk off. "Gotta let Sharkis know anyway."

Chase passed him and turned, walking backward a moment. "No, wait here where you found the bear sign. It's the best place to start, right?" He tossed the question at Winston, didn't wait. "I'll get Lyn, and I'll tell Sharkis. Be back in . . . twenty minutes." He turned and started to jog up trail.

Willis put his hands on his hips and frowned.

Henderson shuffled in the damp earth for a few moments. "I don't want to stand here for twenty minutes."

Allan was watching his father jog away. When he was gone, the boy swallowed hard and spoke in a weak voice, afraid to say these words and terrified to hold them. "He might hurt them."

"What?"

Just a bit louder. "He might hurt them." He began to walk up the trail, following his father.

"What did he say?"

Allan turned to them and stared and summoned all his strength to say again, "He might hurt them."

"You mean Sharkis . . . and your sister?"

Allan nodded. Willis looked at Henderson, and they understood. Without speaking, the three of them turned and moved up the trail in a slogging run.

Til had sent banjo notes showering down the mountain for a full fifteen minutes until he felt he had played Lyn Chase all the way to the resort and into her cabin and flopped her down in a deep, soft chair.

GERALD DI PEGO

Then he sat on the bed and put his feet up, leaned back on the headboard and played more softly, played the girl a love song, then another, then let his fingers loose to roam the strings in a mellow mood and go beyond songs to simple reverie.

His hands, unattached, made music while his mind, drifting, looked over the images of Lyn he had stored like colored slides. He selected one, projected it, chose the next one—fractions of moments, pieces of memory made of smiles and deep stares and full views of a body half turning, a face looking away and then coming around, moving to the sharp clicks of his mind. There she was down in the forest, fallen from her run. Now she swam in the pond. Here she was pointing to the trees, naming them, and the water dripping from her arm was caught and held in space, liquid silver, motionless between her flesh and the surface of the pond.

He took her image beyond memory, into future and fantasy, and he saw her beside him on the bed, eyes closed, shyness gone, peace and pleasure lying soft on her pretty, pretty face.

When the cabin door was rammed open, Til thought for the first half of a second that his mind had grabbed Lyn and pulled her from that soft chair, from her cabin, pulled her up the mountain to his home. In the second half of that second he saw Lou Chase fill his doorway and enter with a rifle thrust before him.

"Where is she!"

Til's fear of the rifle was dissolved in a rush of anger and hate, as if anger and hate could make a shield and the bullets would bounce off. "You didn't knock, asshole." He stood up slowly, leaned the banjo against the wall.

Chase stepped close to him, pointing the rifle from the hip, finger on the trigger. "Where's my daughter?"

"She left." Til heard voices and running bodies outside on the trail, and he heard Lou Chase whisper through clenched teeth.

FOREST THINGS
———

"Then she *was* here."

Lou swung the rifle butt at him.

Til threw his head back but still caught a glancing blow on the jaw. He fell back on the bed, his face afire with pain and rage.

He bounced up from the bed, diving under Chase's second blow and catching the man around the waist, driving him backward to smash against the wall.

Chase raised the rifle to club the bent-over Til, but Til struck now. He punched the man as hard as he could in the belly. Chase crumpled and sat on the floor, dropped the rifle. Til punched him again for Allan, for the purple bruise on the arm of Allan Chase. Chase took the blow on his chest and it nailed him to the floor. Til knelt on him and raised his fist to strike the man for Lyn, for all the blows she had never been able to return—but he was caught from behind and pulled off, struggling in the grip of Stan Willis and Winston Henderson.

"Sharkis!"

Willis had one arm and Winston the other. They wrestled him to the cabin floor. His legs were free, and he sent his kicking boots in search of anything they could find.

"Goddamnit, Sharkis! Roll him over."

Willis handcuffed him and sat him up. Allan stood in the doorway, wide-eyed. Chase struggled to his knees, holding his stomach, fighting for breath to shout, "She was here! *Ask him!*"

"Sharkis?"

"The girl left here half an hour ago! That son of a bitch runs in here with a gun . . ."

"What did you do to her!" Chase got to his feet, snatching up his fallen rifle by the barrel and raising it to smash Til's skull. Willis's back was turned. Allan could only scream, but mean Winston Henderson caught Chase by the back of the neck and sent him down to the floor again.

Winston hulked over the man like a much-used machine,

like the big, battered, Detroit-made, overweight road iron Til always compared him with, and he pointed a scarred and dirty finger at the man and said, "Sharkis wouldn't hurt a little girl."

Willis was pulling Til to his feet, and Til was staring at mean Winston, at bitter, hateful Winston who had surely saved his life.

"Outside. Come on." Willis walked Til ten steps from the cabin.

"What'd you cuff *me* for? He's the crazy . . ."

"Shut up and listen. Where's the girl?"

"She left here half an hour ago to go back to her cabin."

"She isn't there. Nobody's seen her."

"There's a pond . . ."

"They checked."

"Well, I don't know. She took a walk for God's sake!"

"What'd you do to her!" Chase was screaming from the cabin. Winston blocked the doorway. Allan stood just outside, white-faced as a mime, his mouth painted open, eyes afraid.

"Goddamnit, Stan, let me loose. I'll find her."

"We'll go to Rendon's. Henderson!"

Winston stepped out of the doorway.

"I want to separate these two before they kill each other. I'm taking Sharkis down to Rendon's. You three spread out and look for the girl."

"Could be the bear," Winston said. He said it softly so Chase and Allan wouldn't hear.

"He's no killer," Til said.

"Come on." Willis guided Til onto the trail with a hand on his shoulder.

"Winston." Til turned to say thank you, but Winston waved it away.

"Take the cuffs off now."

"No."

They were marching down the trail, and Til felt ashamed—here on his own ground, here in the familiar forest to be so crippled, so wanting in balance. "Why not?!"

"You would've killed 'im."

"He attacked me with a rifle!"

"You would've killed 'im."

"Bullshit."

"You wrecked Clover's diner. Lucky nobody pressed charges."

"The Bergers . . ."

"You, Sharkis. What's going on with you?"

Til walked on, silent.

"Where's the girl?"

"Where's the girl—in the forest! She loves it. She took a walk." He drew in his breath and shouted, cracking the stillness like a trumpet. "Lyn Chase!"

Lyn lay on her stomach, her body nearly upright, clinging to the cliff. Her shoes rested against a slight lip of rock that held her in place. She was dazed. She thought she heard her name called, and she lifted her head to answer. As her weight shifted she lost the lip of rock and slid down.

The boulders below waited to receive her. Rounded and smoothed by ancient ice, they spread like blankets of stone to catch her—but she stopped, fully awake now and digging into the steep mountainside with her fingers, her body, her mind. She willed herself against the dust and rock, made herself part of it, knowing now where she was and what had happened. She moved only her eyes, looking upward and wondering how she could have fallen so far, wondering if she were broken inside and dying; then looking down and recognizing where death was—there, among the boulders.

She slipped ten more inches and gasped and curled her fingers into talons, dug with her toes, her hips, even her face. She was afraid to breathe.

She heard nothing, as if the forest has stopped to watch. She sobbed and then caught her breath again, for a thousand grains of sand were deserting her, sliding from beneath her in tiny avalanches and sprinkling on the rocks below. She breathed softly, short breaths. She searched for roots or handholds and found none to the left. She moved her head carefully to face right and saw nothing but bare rock. She stared at her right hand spread stiff and raised up like a spider. She was no longer conscious of tensing those muscles and directing those fingers. They acted independently. Her body knew it must hold, hold fast or die.

She heard a sound above her and slowly moved her head. It was a trickle of earth and dust, a part of the mountain loosened by her own sliding, giving way to fall down upon her now, strike her face and choke her. She squeezed her eyes closed and sobbed again and slid again, this time crying out as she pushed her fingertips into bare rock, losing flesh, drawing blood.

She stopped, caught for a moment like a drop of water on a window, sure to fall, any second now to obey gravity and slide down and disappear. Her shoes dangled over nothing. She

FOREST THINGS
203

was about to run out of mountain slope. Death was an instant away. There was pain from her fingers, from her forehead, cut and bleeding. There were tears and a great struggle against surrender. Death tempted her like sleep. Just relax, only relax. No more pain. An end to fear. Relax.

But she held, and she tried to call out. She could not draw in very much breath for fear of sliding. Her shout was more of a moan, soft, moist with tears, but it would be enough to direct the searchers. There must be searchers. The woman had seen her fall so of course they were searching—and someone had called her name, or had she imagined it?

They would need to find her very soon, she thought, for she felt only minutes left in her hands and arms, only seconds in the earth and rock beneath her.

Something touched her back, a light, tender touch. Her sweatshirt had been drawn up nearly to her arms by the sliding. Her bare back was feeling the breath of the wind. She heard it now whispering among the trees, building to gusts that hummed through the forest below and above her and made swirls of dust dance up the mountainside. The wind was with her, a welcome hand on her back as she cried out in half a voice and stained the rocks with blood from her fingers and her face.

Til and Willis stomped and banged into the Widow's kitchen as she stared at them, her eyes afraid but ready, prepared for bad news.
"What happened?"
"Just coolin' him off. Sit down, Sharkis."
Til kicked a chair away from the kitchen table and sat on

GERALD DI PEGO

the edge of it, looking at no one. Mrs. Chase had seen them cross the yard, and she hurried to the back door, opened it.

"What's happening?"

"Him and your husband were going at each other so I broke it up. They're on the mountain, lookin' for the girl."

"I should be looking for her," Til said.

"What could've happened?!" Patti looked at each of them, her eyes grabbing them and shaking them, desperate for an answer.

"Likely she just took a walk," Willis said.

The Widow went to the stove. "Everybody sit. I've got coffee here."

"Could it be the bear?!" Patti had been carrying that possibility around for days in some deep drawer of her mind, ever since Lou had shown her the first paw print in the earth. "My God."

"That bear is no killer. Let me go look, Stan. I'll find her in five minutes."

"Why don't you let him go?" Patti said.

The Widow was assembling cups. "Sharkis knows the woods."

"Him and Chase might kill each other."

"Why?!"

"Your daughter was at his cabin . . ."

"She warned me about the hunt, and she left."

The Widow shook her head over the steaming coffee. "Sharkis . . ."

"She left! Now, goddamnit, Stan, I can cover the ground out there better and faster than anybody."

"Are they calling her?" Patti went to the door. "How far could she be?" She went outside. In a moment they heard her shouting her daughter's name.

"One wasn't enough?" The Widow spoke to the cups as she slid them to Willis and to Til. "You had to have everybody in sight?" Now she raised her eyes. "Married women, children . . ."

". . . widows," Til said, completing her list.

FOREST THINGS

The word struck her but she didn't falter. Her face was set with pain and truth. She spoke from a distance, looking out at him from behind two windows of blue glass, dull, smoky blue. "All of us. Everybody. That what you want?" Willis was staring, and she didn't give a damn for him. "Just so it's female. Grab her. Do it. Move on. Like your father before you."

Til stared at the table a moment before he spoke. "How am I supposed to drink this coffee, Edith? Lap it up like some dog, some animal that doesn't talk, some watchdog who takes care of things around here and never says a word?" He was getting louder. "Feed him, give him a clean bed and a list of things to do—the firewood, the stoves and heaters, the motorboat and you."

She brought a fist down hard on the table. Her coffee splashed, and some of the drops landed on her hand. She let them rest there, burning her. Her eyes went bright again, creating a vacuum, sucking blue from everywhere, drawing the color from the blue-willow cups and turning Stan Willis's uniform gray before his eyes. "Yes! Yes, an animal, Sharkis!"

"Yes!" He stood up and kicked his chair back across the room. "But not anymore! Now, goddamnit, turn me loose! I want out of here! I'm going into those woods and I'm going to find that girl!"

"Sit down, Sharkis."

"Stan, I'm beggin' you!"

"Sit down!" Willis retrieved the chair and pushed Til into it. "If they ain't back with her in half an hour, I'm takin' you to town and I'm gonna lock you up."

"Why?!"

"Then I'm comin' back here with men and dogs. We're gonna find the girl and shoot that bear . . ."

"Why lock me up!"

"Because I don't trust you, and I don't think the girl just came and left, not knowin' *you*. What did you do? Is she out there ashamed or scared and hiding? Hah? People don't just disappear out there."

GERALD DI PEGO

206

Til stared at him and then beyond him. He hadn't thought of that. She had run, smiled, turned, disappeared. She had found the same door his father had found twenty-one years ago and stepped through to another place. Gone. The thought chilled him. He fought it. The girl was out there. She *was*.

"Lyn!" Chase drew in an immense breath and bellowed, "Lyn!" in a voice that swept out all of the shadowy corners, searched every place the men could not see.

Allan watched him, saw how he held a hand to his stomach, still hurting from Til's punch. It was unnerving for the boy to see his father hit instead of hitting. He had never seen Lou Chase hit, except in his imagination, in his most secret and sacrilegious daydreams where his father had been pummeled senseless and even killed by him—by Allan.

"Lyn!"

He was sorry for his father—and frightened for Lyn. The family had once owned a cat. At night they would call it, and it would come in from its hunting or climbing or sleeping in the yard. Sometimes they had to call it several times and whistle and click their tongues. One night she did not come at all. They called, waited and called for half an hour. They searched the neighborhood. Concern became worry, worry became dread. They never found her.

Allan felt that dread now.

"Lyn!"

He had stopped expecting to find her. He had lost his faith in that searching voice.

FOREST THINGS
―――――
207

"Lyn!"
The forest felt empty.
"Lyn!"

She slid down by millimeters so that below her knees now was nothing but air. Her thighs and groin cleaved to the earth like a lover. Her stomach and breasts worked to blend with the stone. Her arms and hands were numb with effort, and her fingers had turned to unfeeling steel. Her face, sticky with dried blood, pressed against her mountain pillow, and her mind begged for rest.

She was forgotten. The wind carried no voices to her, no sound of searchers. Searchers would have found her by now. Had the woman fallen too? Had the woman been a dream, a spirit?

Below, the rocks beckoned. They were so hard, so certain. Let go of hope, they said. Let go. Give yourself to us. Rest, Lyn. Close your eyes. Let go.

Her mind was spent. It agreed. It's over, her mind said. It told her body to let go. Her legs and groin refused, breasts and stomach and arms and face only dug deeper into the earth. Her hands didn't even hear, grown deaf and as solid as the mountain. They would not let go until there was no mountain left to hold. She begged her body to stop hoping. She asked the wind to release her. Nothing listened. She held. She slipped by millimeters. The rocks waited.

GERALD DI PEGO

Mag sat on the bed and buried her fingers in her hair. Bats dive for the hair, she had heard. This black bat was diving and screeching closer and closer. She could feel the breath of its wings. She pulled her hair to bring pain and erase all other feelings, but the bat screeched louder. Dead, it screamed. Killed her. Off the cliff. You. Death. Killed her. Lyn Chase.

I didn't. Her mind swatted at the bat. I didn't! She fell. They will find her, and they will say she fell from the cliff, and they will be right. She fell.

Mag stood up and moved stiffly, her body tensed with terror. She lifted her suitcase to the bed, fumbled with the catch, opened it. She searched the cabin for her things and packed them, packed everything, even wrapping the bar of soap in Kleenex and taking two Tilima Lodge brochures and all the matchbooks.

I'll go to town with the hunters. I'll take the bus to Utica and rent a car. I'll drive to to the city, to the apartment, to Michael. I have a life there. I have a job. There is no reason to threaten that, to lose it all.

Killed her, the bat screamed, and outside Patti Chase shouted, "Lyn!"

Mag clenched her trembling hands. She raised them—a doubled fist—and brought them down hard on the bed. Stop, her mind said. "Stop!" she said aloud. She was commanding herself. "Stop. Just . . . stop."

"Lyn!"

Mag breathed deeply and closed her eyes, and she stopped,

FOREST THINGS

stopped running. She had been running since the bus pulled away, running scared, panicked. "Just stop. Stop."

"Twenty-nine," she whispered. "Mag Dermitter. Separated. Attorney. I had an affair. I startled a girl on a mountain path. She fell."

The bat escaped up the chimney.

Patti Chase called her daughter again.

Mag Dermitter rose from the bed and steadied herself.

Willis raised Til's coffee cup and brought it to the man's face. "Want a drink?"

Til didn't answer, didn't look at the man or move his lips to the cup.

"Take him out of here," the Widow said. "Wait somewhere else. Go over to the Chases' cabin. This is no police station."

"This is no social call, Edith. We got a girl missing. We got a rogue bear out there." Willis put the cup down. "The lodge here is headquarters for the search and the hunt."

"Not if I say it isn't. It's my lodge."

"You chasin' me out of here?"

"Yes."

"You're putting the law out of your place?"

"Yes."

"I can commandeer this lodge."

"The hell you can."

"This is official business."

"Do your business outside."

Til jumped from his chair and ran for the door. Willis barreled after him, nearly toppling the table. Til shouldered the screen door out of his way, hit the back porch and stumbled down the stairs. Willis tackled him on the grass of the yard.

They wrestled there. Willis got his bulk on top of Til, but Til kicked him off and rose again.

The Widow watched from her doorway. When Til seemed to be escaping she hurried into the kitchen and then charged outside holding a heavy iron skillet she had snatched off the stove.

Til was down again, but keeping the deputy at bay with his boots. Willis caught one of Til's legs and held on, but the free boot rammed into his shin, and he cursed.

Patti Chase had hurried over and now stood watching, mouth open and hands held out in front of her as if to ward off the wrestlers. She screamed. Til broke free. The Widow raised the skillet like a club. Til dodged. Willis pulled the revolver from his holster. Patti screamed again.

"I startled her and she fell."

Mag's voice halted them because it was so even, so detached from their own chaos—but they hadn't really heard her words, hadn't understood.

"I startled her and she fell off the mountain."

They surrounded her.

"She was coming down the trail and I was going up. I startled her and she fell off a cliff."

Patti moaned a long, hopeless moan.

"Where?!" Til thrust himself at Mag. "What cliff?!" The mountain dropped away from the trail on tree-covered slopes. There was only one spot between the resort and his cabin that could be called a cliff. "Where the mountain is bare stone? Whitestone?"

"Yes."

"Willis!"

Patti cried out again. The Widow dropped her skillet and held the woman from behind, tenderly held her shoulders.

"I was afraid to . . ."

FOREST THINGS

"Willis! The key!" Til turned his back on the deputy. The man pulled out his keys, glancing at Mag as he freed Til.

"You'll show us where."

"Yes, I . . ."

Once free, Til bounded away, hopping once and then racing toward the forest.

"Sharkis! Wait!"

The searchers had made a wide circle around Til's cabin, gone halfway up to the top of Tilima, down again, ranging through the woods, wasting their voices a full half-mile from Whitestone cliff. As they reached the trail again, Henderson glanced down the slopes and searched the distant face of Whitestone but saw nothing, no one.

"Might as well head back."

"No." Chase led them on, moving across level land now.

"Lyn never came this way," Allan said.

"So what." Chase felt she might be hiding, watching, punishing him. He hated her for that. He thought also she might have been raped by Til or at least seduced by him and now was wandering the forest shaken and ashamed, and if so, he loved her and pitied her, and he hoped for a chance to kill Til Sharkis.

Chase, Henderson and Allan had spread wide apart. Allan heard the sound first—swift movement through the forest, muffled by the wind, then clear again. The boy carried the .22 revolver holstered at his hip. He had put it on for the bear hunt, for protection, for signaling, for the feeling that he was truly part of the adventure. He now unsnapped the leather

GERALD DI PEGO

guard and touched the handle. Something heavy, something fast, was making its way toward him. It did not seem to be running on human legs. It came on the wind. He remembered the sight of the bear only ten steps ahead of him on the trail, remembered the claws. He drew the gun. The thing would be in sight any second, unless it was invisible and passing him right now. The wind rushed and moaned, gusting hard, the boy's eyes snapped about, watchful, ready.

It was here. He raised the gun. It was Til—running, leaping, flying through the forest. Allan watched him pass, never thinking to speak, for the man was not running on human legs and so not capable of speech or thought. He was a thing of the forest. A man could not run that fast with so little sound, with so little stirring of the woods. Allan watched the forest thing with awe and with longing until it was gone.

"Who is that?!" He heard his father call. Then the man screamed, "Sharkis! It's Sharkis! Hey! *Stop!*"

The man fired. The deer rifle punctured the sky and punished the forest with its echo.

Allan screamed, "Dad! No!"

"Chase, what're you . . . !"

Lou Chase had fired into the air. He screamed, "Stop!" again and then lowered his sights on the running man, swinging the gun to lead him like a bird.

"Daddy!"

But Til was lost among the trees.

"Get him," Chase screamed, and he ran after the man, drawing Allan and Henderson with him.

FOREST THINGS

Til could hear them behind him, and his back tingled, expecting a bullet, but he ran on, his legs springing, leaping yards, rolling acres of ground behind him. He could see the bare white clifftop above the trees and he aimed his body toward it. His legs flew him there, his feet never tangling, barely touching, his arms shoulder-high for balance, his face set. He was running with purpose today, running for speed, running for Lyn.

He was sending the last of the lowland trees behind him, reaching the base of the cliff, searching the boulders as he ran, afraid to see her bloody and broken there. His eyes were drawn up to a dark spot on the cliff face, sixty feet up, just below the great white pine. He slid to a stop. It was her, dangling over nothing, holding to a slight outcropping of rock, pinioned there only by the wind, attached only by her fingers and the desperate embrace of her body and the mountainside.

He ran again, mounting the boulders like a goat, charging the steep hillside and willing himself up, up to her.

She heard sounds struggling to rise above the moaning of the wind, a scuffling, a voice but not a human voice, a beast at work, grunting, breathing below her. "Lyn!" The beast spoke. "Lyn!" It wept.

GERALD DI PEGO

Oh, God, now, she told her body, hold now. Hold. Yes, hold.

He swept up the mountainside on a great gust of wind, using every lump of earth and edge of rock. He found a dent in the cliff twenty feet below her where he could stand securely. There was no way to climb any further.

"Drop," he said.

She cried out in relief and fear, hope and terror. Drop. She had used every cell in her body to stay up. Dropping was death.

"Drop to me."

She ordered her fingers to let go. They did not move.

"Lyn!"

This was Til beneath her. It was all right. She could let go. Her fingers, her body refused. She began to cry. Her crying loosened the last of the earth that held her. She fell.

He caught her and they fell to their knees on the narrow ledge. They embraced, and her body began to loosen, to become flesh again and to feel the arms and heaving chest of Til. He put his face to hers. They laughed and wept. When they drew back, she saw the image from her dream. Half of Til's face was coated with blood—her blood. He smiled through the blood, kissed her through the blood.

They eased down the mountainside, jumped to the highest of the boulders. She was shaking now, her arms and hands aching. He lowered her to the ground and held her, kneeling beside her.

The wind softened, died, and through the forest came the sounds of men, a great rushing and crashing, heavy boots, a gun fired into the sky.

Birds scattered. A rabbit dodged behind the boulders. Chipmunks darted for the deepest shadows, and Til picked up the girl and ran for the trees.

Even with Lyn in his arms he could run. Behind him, the shouts and footsteps of the men prodded him, drove him. Ahead, he was welcomed by the big pine and fir who made

FOREST THINGS

shadows for him, by the beech, maple and birch who screened him from the sight of the hunters.

"Til!"

His arms were dragging down now and his legs moved more slowly, striking the ground heavily. The girl was struggling in his arms and calling out. It was over.

"Til. Til, I can run. I can."

He stared at her, slowly lowering her, unbelieving. She smiled at him with wonder and wondrous courage, and then she ran—ahead of him, away from the men, forward among the forest things. He caught up and ran beside her. They leaped fallen trunks and raced between the trees, flowing with every dip and turn of land, barely touching the forest floor.

They took flight.

GERALD DI PEGO